NATASHA KARIS

The Three Stories For Vicky Fitzgerald

First published by Diamond Roads 2025

First edition

ISBN: 978-1-8380652-8-7

Proofreading by Sian Phillips
Cover art by Jellytots Design

This book was professionally typeset on Reedsy.
Find out more at reedsy.com

For my Nan, Mary McCarthy.
And all the relatives who came before.
Your blood runs through mine.
Your wisdom runs through each page.
The traits you taught your children filters down and carries on.
Nan, I see you in my daughters' face.
I still feel your love.

Contents

Playlist

I Put A Spell On You by IZA
Headstones And Landmines by Lizzie McAlpine
Poor Boy's Shoes by Declan O'Rourke
Everything I Wanted by Billie Eilish
Take Me To Church by Hozier
Buried In The Deep by Declan O'Rourke
Same Boat by Lizzie McAlpine
Too Good At Goodbyes by Sam Smith
Let It Go by James Bay
The Sailor's Bonnet by The Gloaming
https://youtube.com/playlist?
list=PLXUprm9AeVXeXw9WQ5SFKNa0b7wyAIHlx&
si=QEExrBSkzw6Ie3hA

Prologue

A flash of light. A crack of thunder. Cold water hitting bones. Ringing in ears and a sharp throbbing in her forehead where she was hit. Worse still, worse than anything else ever, he is gone. And she knows, *she knows*, before she sees, before his absence is determined by facts that confirm, her life has forever changed.

He is lost to her.

And with him gone, any reason to want to go on leaves too. She will not recover from this. From now on, she will view life as a cruel master of fate. A fate she has no control over. From now on she will only exist. Only survive. In an instant, the light inside her extinguishes.

Chapter 1

Before children stuffed their faces after trick or treating, or the streets filled with advancing ghouls and goblins, witches and pirates, Sergeant Vicky Fitzgerald walked through the park in the biting wind on the hunt for some eggs. Or, closer to the truth, the throwers of some eggs. If she listened to the urge to look up, the surrounding trees would have made her gasp; every colour of leaf present, dancing to the winds beat. Too focused on the task at hand, she kept her eyes on the ground, for the last thing she needed tonight was to fall headfirst into muck. Even so, Vicky couldn't miss the colours as her feet landed on crimson, pumpkin and rust, the satisfying crunch lost from the light drizzle of rain that started an hour ago.

Locating the three boys didn't take long. All she needed to do was stand still, cock the ear, and follow the roars that lifted above the wind. The boys weren't original, hiding in the most obvious place teenagers could go; seeking shelter from the unrelenting nip of wind behind the only building in the park.

'All right, boys?' she asked as she rounded the corner.

'My heart,' one boy muttered, although he didn't move from his squatting position on the floor.

Another one shuffled, taking a sidestep left, then right, as if he considered bolting then thought better, which awarded him a good start in Vicky's eyes as she didn't fancy chasing someone around a park tonight. Also, they both knew it would be pretty futile when she knew where he lived. The other boy, looking more like an adult for the height of him, the main one to watch, shoved his hands in the pocket of his hoodie, creating a lumpy shape around his stomach, as if he was holding or hiding something there. Moving from squatting to sitting, he kicked his legs out, stabbing the air with his feet, in an act of defiance, saying without saying, *I'm not afraid of you.*

She didn't speak either, for Vicky found silence could be very effective with the guilty when they're dying to unburden. With hands on her hips, she made a point of surveying the scene. It wasn't a pretty sight. Littered by their feet lay flattened cans, disposable vapes, abandoned lighters, dubious discarded rollie ends alongside definite cigarette butts. She suppressed a shudder at what looked like a used condom.

Vicky knew these boys like she knew everyone in the town. It was her job to, and in a small place like Knockfarraig, it was easy.

'Tell me, what are ye up to for the night?'

'It's Halloween, so we'll be doing Halloween stuff probably, Garda.'

'It's Sergeant, actually.'

The boys looked at her with blank stares. She rolled her eyes, then pointed at the cans.

'What's drinking got to do with Halloween?'

The boy, Billy, nearly sixteen, dangled the can high so she could see, as if that was an answer in itself.

She shrugged, shook her head. When that didn't bring a conclusion, she spoke. 'Yeah? So?'

Billy held the can closer to her, as if seeing it properly would sort out her confusion.

'Cider.'

She wrinkled her forehead, circled her hand to encourage him to elaborate.

He wiggled the can at the same speed as his head, making a "duh face" as if she was stupid. 'Everyone knows you do stuff with apples at Halloween.'

'Wow, that's genius.' She folded her arms. 'What other Halloween stuff are you planning, then?'

There was silence. The other two boys kept their heads down. For once, Billy stayed quiet, too. Vicky almost laughed at their naivety; they believed they were streetwise, yet the guilt came off them in waves.

'Would the Halloween stuff include egging cars or, in particular, buses then?'

The penny dropped with Billy. Instead of being scared, he stood up, stepped towards her.

'It's Halloween. It's practically the law to egg things.'

In hostile situations, only making herself bigger would do. Becoming angular, her hands landed on her hips again. Vicky stood as tall as she could, expanded herself out to the maximum space she could take up, matching Billy's bravado.

'Did you have to boil them, though? Those eggs were rock hard. They could've smashed through the window or taken an eye out.'

Billy edged closer. The fifteen-year-old was already taller, which was saying something, as Vicky was taller than most at five-eleven. This teen was heading past six feet.

'Prove it.'

Vicky didn't flinch. Her face didn't change one bit. She took a step back, appraising him. His runners were a concoction of rubber shapes, probably cost more than her whole wardrobe. The tracksuit was the same. Full of squiggles, the brand name muted but still there. She kept her tone non-threatening.

'I like your style. Makes you stand out. Looks expensive ... quite unusual. Rare even, I'd say.'

The other teen cottoned on, standing up and elbowing Billy, but the talker continued anyway. Not always the brightest spark, he led with his mouth and Vicky had found in the past if you pushed past his bark, the bite never came. There was always a first time though, bravado grows from causing trouble and things can change in an instant. From the amount of cans flung around, the possibility of him becoming more agitated than usual was there.

'Limited edition. Cost a fortune,' he said with pride, flicking at the hoodie's material.

'Well, that alone will get you a night in the cell. Makes you easily identifiable. Won't be hard to spot now that CCTV is on every bus, especially when the driver described exactly those clothes.'

Billy rubbed at his nose then, acting unbothered, drained the can. 'That station is a joke. It's just for show. Everyone knows it closes at night.'

She shrugged.

'Doesn't have to stay closed. Having the keys, I can always throw a messer in there if I choose. Heard it gets pretty spooky at night, especially if you're alone. Ever hear the history of the place? Rumour has it many a prisoner died from a beating down in the basement. That's where we keep drunk teens when they need to sleep off their behaviour. Now, I'm used to the station but even I wouldn't fancy staying there on Halloween. Any of ye a believer in ghosts? Wanna put that bravery to the test?'

Billy automatically shivered, then brazened up, flinging the can on the ground. Vicky considered how to win this argument while giving Billy some saving grace.

'Now, I just came over here to give you a heads up on how your night will go if you carry on doing the things you've been doing tonight, 'cos I'm hoping I don't have to go through the paperwork and hassle of getting a cell ready and would much prefer to be twiddling my thumbs at home with a hot chocolate reading a book an hour from now. What I recommend is you do the same. No one got hurt. This time. Luckily, it didn't smash the glass and the bus driver saw the funny side and doesn't want to pursue anything, but you see how the night could turn out if this kind of behaviour continues? Your choice, Billy. What's it going to be?'

Judging by the boy's expression, it was going to be a long night. The wind let out a roar, making the four of them look above.

The leaves fell from the sky like snow. Red and brown leaves flurried and bustled, whirling in circles in the air. The fading light made it a stunning sight, yet its beauty held a threat. In Ireland storms were an occasion a few times a year, if any, and when she could, Vicky tried to stay indoors. The nature of the job meant there were instances she couldn't refuse, as much as the sanctuary of the station appealed. Out in the distance, the sea loomed black and threatening. It would not stay still tonight.

'It's meant to get rough tonight, lads. Better for everyone if you head home. There's a storm coming.'

'Vicky, come in, Vicky.'

Phyllis's shaky voice transported through the walkie talkie speaker. Vicky checked the time, then took a few paces away from the lads.

'Phyllis, I thought you'd packed up for the afternoon. You don't have to stay on remember? Just divert to my phone and I'll work from that.'

'That's what I was doing. The phone went only this minute as I was walking out the door and I thought it was better to let you know straight away as it's a strange one. It was Ruth, down on Main Street. You know Ruth? The woman who had the twins, the boy and the girl that—'

'I know who Ruth is, Phyllis. What did she call you about?'

Phyllis huffed. She hated being interrupted in the middle of a juicy story.

'There's an old man standing in the middle of main street and he's blocking all the cars from getting past and you know they're meant to start the Samhain parade at four on the dot and it's three-thirty now and—'

'Don't worry, I'll go there right away.' She glanced at the teens, clocking their relief, their eyes wide with the possibility of freedom.

'Vicky?'

'Yeah?'

'Just so you know …'

Vicky prepared herself to interrupt. Inherited with the station, Phyllis, for the most part, was a sympathetic listener when a distressed caller rang, a kind colleague who made sure Vicky ate, and an adequate secretary, but she sure liked to ramble.

'… the old man is as naked as the day he was born.'

'Christ,' Vicky groaned. 'Probably someone from the old folks' home or something. All right, look, I'm on it. Lock up for me and I'll see you tomorrow.'

'The station is closed tomorrow and the next day, remember? You won't see me before Wednesday.'

'Right. See you then.'

Even though her instinct was to rush off, Vicky slowed her gestures down, then turned to the boys, who weren't even trying to conceal their grins. Time for the talk.

'You think you've got away with this, right? Well, know this before you go. You've probably heard many things about me, like I'm a loner, or a bitch, or a weirdo, or I don't have a life outside being a sergeant. All of those things are right. Which means even though the station should be closed, even though I'm only meant to work till …' she checked her watch, '… an hour ago. I like to keep working. In fact, I've nothing to do but work, so I've all the time in the world to find you later and, Billy, I will if I hear you're causing any more trouble. Or you, Conor.'

Conor straightened up; his eyes wide with the realisation she knew his name.

'Or you, Oran. Just because you keep quiet it doesn't mean my eye isn't on both of you either.'

The two boys stared at the floor.

'If I gave ye a body search right now, I've a funny feeling I'd find more than sweet wrappers. There's more than one cell down there. Remember that and stay out of trouble. Right?'

'Right,' they chorused.

She shook her head, enjoying the conversation now. 'Cans.'

They didn't move. She held out her hand then wiggled her fingers. 'You hardly thought I was going to let you carry on drinking now, did ye?'

With reluctance, the boys gathered up their stash and handed it over.

'You teens ... you think you're the first people on earth to push boundaries. All it makes you is dumb. You haven't an original thought in your head. Do you know what's impressive? Being able to hold your head up high when you look your mother in the eye. Seeing her face when you pass your exams, when you tell her you landed a job, when you hand over a piece of your first pay packet. You have no clue what pride feels like. Now, that is something to aim for.'

She sighed.

'Billy, come here.'

Striding towards the corner, she gestured for him to follow. He did what he was told, albeit slowly. Vicky halted when she was certain they were out of hearing range.

'How's your mam?'

Billy shifted. The shock on his face at the question was a picture. He didn't answer.

'I'm serious. How's your mam getting on with the treatment?'

He shrugged, kicked at the ground. 'Grand, I suppose.'

'She's not long into it. You've got to be strong for her, you know? Before she can get better, the treatment will be tough. Has her hair started falling out?'

He wouldn't look at her, just shook his head instead. The kicking stopped, and he hunched his back lower.

'You only get one mam, Billy. I know. Lost mine very young, when

I was about your age and I'll tell you now, what I wouldn't do to have a word with her.' She leant her back against the wall. 'A hug actually, I'd give anything for a hug. You have *your* mam. What do you think it would do to her if I pulled up outside your house in a squad car with you inside?'

This made him look up. 'Don't.'

'If I thought it would teach you a lesson—'

He cut the air with his hands. 'I'm taught, Guard, I'm taught, there's no need.'

'Here's what we both know.' She held a finger up. '*I* know you've been underage drinking.' She held another finger up. 'I also know you've stuff in your pockets.' A third finger rose. 'While *you* know hitting buses with eggs is a serious offence. What if Gretta had been on that bus and it crashed, Billy?'

His eyes widened.

She nodded. 'Yeah, I used to know your mam real well. Held you when you were a baby and, as far as kids go, you were cute enough. No one looked at a child with as much love as her. She didn't deserve the way your dad treated her. You didn't either.'

Even with his head down, Vicky saw his eyes water.

'Don't repeat his mistakes. Take after the good in your family, leave the bad behind. I don't want to see you again tonight. Right?'

He nodded; his head stayed down.

'Okay then, one chance. For your mother. Now, go home and give her that hug.'

She walked away without checking over her shoulder, even though she stayed on alert in case an empty can vaulted near her head. Always ready to react, even if it looked like the words sank in with Billy, Vicky was always ready for the worst unfolding. On this occasion, the boy didn't risk it.

Halfway across the park, her mind shifted to who stood on Main Street.

Why was there a man naked? The wind blasted her with enough force she had to grab her hat to keep it in place.

Already, she knew, it was going to be a long night.

Chapter 2

For once, Phyllis wasn't exaggerating. There, in the middle of the street, right in the middle of the town, stood a man with all his bits on display. Vicky had witnessed many strange sights in her career, but an old man without clothes on was a first, so, for a moment, she forgot professionalism. From behind, the man's skin hung loose from the bone, thin and creased like crepe paper.

How could skin end up that far away from where it started?

A blast of wind slapped away her hesitation, forcing her into movement. Thankful the glare and position of the cars blocked the man's full frontal, for *that* was a sight nobody needed to see, Vicky edged forwards.

The man showed signs of being startled. He kept turning slightly to the left, then right. Catching a glimpse at his face, no agitation seemed present, rather, the man acted confused, lost even, or afraid, like an animal startled by an oncoming car. She tapped at the window of the nearest driver, Greg from the bakery, until he wound it down.

'Turn off your lights.'

After Greg did as he was told, she gestured to the next car, and the next until the other drivers cottoned on, doing the same. Noticing what was happening, the old man stopped turning, his loose skin taking a little longer to catch up until he was facing her. She wouldn't look down, keeping eye contact she didn't rush, allowing the man to take in her slow movement. She raised her arms a little, palms out, blocking her view but also she found it was the best way to show she was non-threatening and had nothing to hide, or wasn't holding a weapon, the gesture being an unspoken, universal sign for: *hold on, everything's going to be fine, I'm here to help.*

It had the right effect. Instead of panicking, the old man's worried expression lifted, changed completely even, as if genuinely delighted to see her. Witnessed too many times, Vicky understood it was the sight of her uniform. When someone needed help, after any distress, a Garda's presence instilled an instant comforting effect, signalling to a victim their trauma had ended. Unfortunately, Vicky knew otherwise, the ordeal ended with the Garda's arrival, but trauma hung around or made its appearance long after. Trauma never left straight away; it continued until the person refused to hold on to it any longer. Meaning sometimes, too often, it never disappeared.

Vicky shook off her jacket as she approached; there was a bite to that increasing wind. If she could feel it, an old man could definitely catch a cold.

'Everything all right, sir?'

He opened and closed his mouth. Vicky edged closer, holding the jacket out. The old man stared at the offering, his brows knitted together, as if he hadn't a clue what the jacket was for.

'It's freezing out here tonight. Will you put this on for me and then we can get you home?'

'Home,' the old man repeated. He looked right at her. His eyes were bright-blue. Surprisingly alert, betraying his jittering body.

'Yes, home.'

For a long time, he didn't move, just stood in the one spot, staring. If Vicky was the kind of person that scared easily, it might have caused unease. Instead, it put her on guard, for something wasn't right with this man. The way he was looking at her was off. Not in a plea for help, or a disoriented attempt at trying to figure out who she was, for as ridiculous as it was it seemed like the opposite of that, for the old man was looking at Vicky as if he knew her, as if he recognised her. Which was impossible. Vicky never forgot a face, and she was certain she had never laid eyes on this man before. She *definitely* didn't know him.

Shaking the jacket to get his attention, she pointed the nearest sleeve closer. Without a fight, he slipped an arm in, then she wrapped the jacket around, sliding his other arm through. He stood without movement, without gathering it to his body. Like you would do with a child, she stuck the Velcro together, being careful not to catch any bits of skin in the zip, avoiding looking down. Once she reached the top, she was relieved the jacket reached his mid-thigh. Now that the coat saved his modesty, and he wasn't in danger of dropping down with pneumonia, Vicky could evaluate the rest of the situation.

Prevented from moving on, cars backed up on both sides of the road. Quite a crowd had gathered to see an old man naked out on the street. Vicky spotted Darren Dean standing on the pavement.

'You didn't think of giving the man your coat?' she shouted.

'He's grand with you now, Vicky, but he was livid a minute ago. If anyone even went near, he started punching. Anyway, I don't think this leather jacket would do much for him now, do you?'

It was true. Darren's short bomber jacket was worn for fashion rather than protection from the rain and would barely reach the end of the man's chest. It was hard to believe the docile fellow standing before her would act like that, but Darren was a decent sort with no need to lie.

She leaned in, so she could speak near the man's ear. 'How about we get you off the road so we can find out how to help?'

The old man hung his head with none of the fighting spirit Darren spoke about. She steered him off the road towards Darren.

'What's your name?'

His mouth gaped, then closed, his eyes watered, but that wasn't surprising; the wind whipped at their hair and faces. All the while he stared, as if lost for words. She patted his arm.

'Don't worry, we'll figure it all out. Let me just get this traffic moving and the crowd to stop gawking. Will you stand with Darren here for a minute? He's a bit of an idiot who believes he's a rock star, but harmless enough.'

She said the last bit low, but not low enough for Darren not to hear. She winked at him in apology. Darren was actually sound; they'd grown up in the same circles and lived in Knockfarraig all their life together; he'd understand she was just trying to get the man on side.

'No worries, I'll look after you.'

Darren laid a hand on the man's shoulder, flashing a new tattoo between his thumb and forefinger. A twisty design which probably meant something profound, knowing Darren. The next time she met him she'd make a point of admiring it as a peace offering. At this stage, the only part of Darren that wasn't covered in ink was his face. His music was good too, ranging from soulful to rock. His voice could stop you in your tracks; husky tones with the power to distract you from your problems and keep you present for a second.

The old man didn't put up any fight. He stood with his arms loose by his sides as Vicky dispersed the crowd, moving along the traffic, telling the locals there was nothing to see. Trying to move the standers was futile as, with the parade starting soon, they had the perfect excuse to stay.

'Are you cut anywhere?' she asked when she returned.

He followed her gaze downwards and lifted his foot in answer. Acted surprised, as if he only just realised he was barefoot. Once she checked the first one, she repeated the same with the other until satisfied his soles were unharmed.

'No need for stitches. Let's keep it that way. I'd like to bring you over to my car and we can have a chat there? That way I can turn the heating on.'

The man acted unsure, casting his eye over both sides of the street.

'You'd make me feel better if I knew there was less chance of any harm coming to you. Please, just sit in the car with me.'

Those blue eyes flashed at her again. An unusually bright shade, almost turquoise. Pockets of skin folded and puckered around the corners and under each eye, giving him a harmless, docile expression, reminding her of a pug. At a guess, the man's age was late eighties or older even, yet his movements on the street, the force of how he twisted, made him appear younger, or fitter, than the average person of that age. He stared again with that same look from earlier, as if he knew something, as if he knew her. This made Vicky more uncomfortable than if he pulled punches.

As gently as she could, she turned him toward the other side of the road, then pointed at the car.

'We'll only go as far as there. We don't have to drive, just sit and talk, get some heat into your bones. Don't know about you, but I could do with warming up. That wind could slice right through a body.'

When the man walked, he didn't lift his legs. Yet it wasn't a shuffle either. Almost like his feet scraped the ground. Vicky winced at what damage that could do to his skin. The priority was getting him to the car, though, where she could lock the door and keep him safe. Later, she could bandage feet.

As she opened the passenger door, he grabbed her by both arms, holding onto her with a strength of someone much younger. She cursed her stupid presumptions. With Billy, or anyone else, she would never let her guard down. Even though his grip was tight, tight enough to not loosen easily, he seemed to only want her attention, her eye contact.

'Don't leave me in there.'

'I won't do anything to you. All I want is to get you warm and find out how I can help. You aren't in any trouble; you're not being arrested or anything like that. There must be people out there worried about you now and I want to do my best to reunite you with them.'

His grip stayed.

'You won't believe what I have to say. You never believe people.'

His words cut through Vicky. Many people, on too many occasions, had repeated that last line, the most recent being only earlier today from the superintendent. Always, every time before, she dismissed those comments, but there was something about this stranger, this man, that made her stop.

'What did you say?'

'You won't believe me. You must trust people. Vicky, you need to listen.'

She scanned the dashboard to see if she had left something out with her name on it. Had Darren or one of the crowd called her by her name? Or mentioned to the man who she was before she arrived? Whatever it was, the man was more alert than it first appeared.

She spoke clearly, her tongue rolling over every word.

'I promise I will listen to you. Can we just get into the car?'

The man let go, his arms hanging loose again. She cupped his head softly as he stepped in, making sure it didn't hit the door's roof. Once closed, she took a breath. Safe now; confined. Kids and adults gathered on both sides of the street. Skeletons and monsters, witches and fairies lined up alongside each other.

'More money than sense,' she muttered, shuddering as she spotted one with an all too realistic pig's head. She climbed into the front seat of the car and turned the engine on.

'Let's get some heat into you first before we have a chat.'

Warm air blasted out. She closed her eyes for a second as she felt it pass over her body. Vicky hadn't realised how cold she was until the tightness from her bones subsided.

A spooky reaper came up close to the window, startling her.

'When did Halloween get so commercial? Trick or treating wasn't a thing when I was a kid. I imagine it wasn't for you either?'

No response.

Vicky searched the black sky, listened to the howl of wind.

'They'll be lucky if they get ten minutes of the parade before the rain comes. If there's one thing I'd put money on, it's that it always rains on Halloween.'

She glanced at the man. His head was tilted, jaw up, leaning on the headrest, with his eyes closed.

'Are you unwell? Do you need anything?'

He fluttered his eyes, shook his head.

Quick Dementia test.

'Before I listen, can you just answer a few questions so I'm sure you aren't unwell?'

He nodded.

'Do you know where you are?'

'Knockfarraig.'

'Do you know the date?'

'It's the thirty-first of October. Samhain.'

'We've already established you know my name. Can I just confirm you know yours?'

'I know my name.'

'Want to share it?'

'Not until you're ready to listen.'

She drummed her nails against the steering wheel. 'I could drive us to a petrol station and get you a tea? Or to your home?'

He stayed silent. His scowl stronger than any word.

'That's right, I'm meant to listen. Well, I'm all ears if you want to talk. Just wanted to check if you wanted a hot drink, that's all.'

The old man looked out the window and watched the line of children and parents. He pointed at the glass, looking back at her with confusion.

'They are getting ready for the parade; it's starting in a minute. When it does, it will get loud, we might not hear each other with all the floats and performance artists on the street. Might be best to move away now, otherwise we'll be stuck here until all the people disperse.'

A Dracula cloak hit the side of the window.

'This wind will keep most people indoors, though. The weather reports got it wrong; this storm won't pass us by like they made out. It's only going to get wilder.'

The sea threatened. If the waves broke the walls around the beach, the streets that ran parallel to the beach could flood. Plenty of people might need shelter tonight, need to be evacuated.

He nodded his consent to move.

'If you don't want to go far, there's a petrol station up the road?'

He shrugged in answer.

'Good. I didn't fancy listening to screeches and wails. They're planning an enactment of calling the dead for Samhain.'

He nodded again. 'Samhain, I know.'

The rain came then, as forceful as if the heavens opened and threw buckets on the ground. She pulled out and drove, then splayed a hand in his direction, to indicate she was listening. It didn't take the old man long.

'Hearing about ghosts in the old tales, you would never want to imitate them. Growing up, they were not something to be laughed about.'

'Same.' She smiled; glad he was sharing. 'My father used to gather us around the fire on Halloween and tell us the stories, the Irish folklore. I was glad to hear the parade this year was a Samhain celebration, bringing back our traditions. All we hear about these days is Halloween.'

The old man edged closer. 'You know Samhain?'

She chuckled at his surprise and slowed the car down to see out, the rain blocking her view.

'I know all about Samhain. The one positive thing my dad did was ingrain it into me as a kid.'

She tapped her temple. 'The details are muddled but I kept the gist of them all. There was a time I could recite the stories verbatim. Not tales for kids, really. Most kept me up half the night. You accused me of not trusting people, well, I'd blame those tales. The distrust started there. Like, Jack O'Lantern, banished from heaven *and* hell, forced to roam the earth for all eternity, not exactly a happy ending. That kind of story has you reaching for a weapon in the middle of the night.'

'There were other stories, too.'

'Yeah, lots, like I said, the kind that keeps you up.'

'No!'

Vicky braced at the outburst. She gripped the steering wheel for composure, then turned into the petrol station. Parking, she glanced at him.

The man was rubbing his face, tossing his hair, agitated.

'We're here now. I can give you my full attention,' she said in a soft voice.

His shoulders dropped, his face earnest.

'You're too quick to judge.'

She smiled. 'Habit of the job. *For* the job. Believe it or not, it serves me well to assess a situation quickly.'

'Not always correctly.'

She bristled. 'I do what I can.'

'When I was a child, we respected the dead. Saw them as sacred. We opened our doors, saw Samhain as a gift. Treating them with kindness meant the crops would live. We would live. Now it's all a joke.'

Crops? Who spoke like that anymore?

'Would you like a coffee or a tea?'

He tilted his head. 'See, you still don't listen.'

'Will you at least tell me your name?'

The man folded his arms, stared out the window.

Don't push. Listen.

'Look, I haven't eaten since this morning. Give me a second to refuel, then you can have my undivided attention.'

Under the shelter of the petrol station roof, it didn't offer any protection from the rain. The droplets hit her clothes from all directions and, minus a jacket, soaked her shirt in seconds. As she dashed into the cover of the petrol station's shop, making sure the man couldn't see her hands, she did a quick search on her phone for all the residential homes near Knockfarraig. For such a small town, there were three. Surely, they couldn't all be full of the town's elderly? Must be out-of-towners wanting to ease the guilt of kicking their mums or dads from their own house by sending them to a place near the sea.

Dialling the first number, she waited. A woman picked up on the third ring.

'Seaview residential home. How can I help?'

Seaview. Definitely out of towners.

'Hi, this is Vicky Fitzgerald, the sergeant here in Knockfarraig. I'm just calling to check if you're missing a patient there?'

'Resident.'

'Sorry?'

'We do not class them as patients; we call them residents here.'

Vicky spoke through gritted teeth. 'Patient, resident, whatever. Are you keeping check of the people that pay you to watch over them?'

'Every hour on the hour.'

'You sure about that? Because I just picked up a naked man from the middle of the street and I don't think it would look good if you missed one of your ... residents.'

The woman's tone changed, relented. 'Let me just do a quick scan on the computer and check with my manager.'

'Do that.'

Vicky put the call on hands free while she poured the hot water. She looked at the unappetising pastries, most of which looked deflated and soggy.

'What do old people like to eat? Soft, I guess, in case they have dentures,' she said to herself.

She picked up a packet of dry biscuits. 'Perfect for dunking.'

Approaching the counter, she pointed at the hot food. 'Hey, Doreen, will you throw some sausages in a bag for me?'

'Hello? Hello?'

Vicky pointed at the phone so Doreen would know she had to take it, then stepped away to let the person behind her take her place.

'Hi ... sorry, had to take you off speaker. Go ahead, I can talk now.'

'Garda Fitzgerald, I checked through the system and everyone is accounted for. One man often likes to go walkabout, so we checked him in person to be sure, but he's sat in our tearoom sipping a hot chocolate as we speak.'

'Right, that's good ... for you, anyway. You have my number if it turns out you're wrong?'

'I do, but I won't be. We keep a thorough eye on our residents here.'

Vicky dismissed the pride in the woman's voice, proud people often let their emotions distract from the truth.

'That's what you're paid for, though, right?'

'Goodnight, Garda Fitzgerald,' the woman answered before the phone clicked off.

Vicky dialled the other two numbers, but they rang out unanswered. Not wanting to delay any longer, she walked back to the car after paying Doreen. The old man was staring right at her. The way he looked at the phone, then at her, with such sadness, with disappointment even, unnerved her. She shoved the phone back in her pocket. The other places could wait.

It was time to listen to what the man had to say.

Chapter 3

Vicky handed him a tea, keeping the coffee for herself, then cupped her fingers around the welcome hot drink.

'Isn't it funny how last night it was warm and then one night later, everything changes? Isn't that what Halloween is, the winter coming in?'

'Samhain is. It means summer's end *as gaeilge*, I know nothing of this Halloween business.'

She twisted to face him in the back. 'It's good to see you've found your voice. The tea help?'

He nodded, blowing at the steam while cupping it in his hands.

'Ready to tell me your name?'

He looked out the window. Shook his head slowly.

'You sure you remember?'

He stared at her, but no words came. The wind picked up again, and the car shook with the force.

'It's getting worse out there. We can't stay in the car all night, it's not safe. You asked me to listen, but you're not talking much.'

'Not here.'

She made an exaggerated check of the empty seats.

'Why? There's no one else around. No one to listen to what you have to say. Why would you need to be so nervous, anyway? What does it matter?'

'It matters to you.'

She chuckled. 'How's that now? Are you going to confess to a load of cold case crimes that are doing my head in?' She clicked her fingers. 'I know, you're the garden-pot robber that's been tormenting Mrs Leahy! You've been keeping me up all night trying to crack that one.'

The rain lashed on the window as if in protest at her poor joke. The force made it impossible to see out. The man didn't seem to notice, just kept looking right at her.

'It matters because you care about people. You care, but you're afraid to trust anyone. You're afraid to love.'

Vicky dropped the smile. 'You don't know me, sir.'

One corner of his mouth rose, not goading, seeming sincere. 'I know more than you think. That's all I'll say here.'

'You can't make a statement like that and then go silent.'

A lapse in the rain gave a view again. The trees in the distance violently bent one way, then shifted in the other direction.

'This isn't the place to talk, there are too many distractions outside. You're right, it isn't safe. If I'm talking, telling you my story, I need to see you. I need to watch your reaction,' he said.

'If you didn't know already, I found you in the middle of the street, starkers. All you *need* is to remember where you live so I can drop you home. And judging by the strength of this storm, it needs to be pretty quickly.'

The old man turned his head towards the window, his mouth closed in a straight line.

She pinched the bridge of her nose, closed her eyes and took a deep breath. *Wrong move, Vicky.*

'Can you at least tell me if you had a fall of some kind?'

He stayed silent.

'Right then,' she said, pulling out. 'We need to get you checked for a concussion or a brain injury or something. I'm taking you to the hospital.

If you can't say how you got here, I'll have them tell me.'

'Don't,' he said, so low she could barely hear.

'What was that?' She continued driving.

'Don't. There's nothing wrong with me. If you bring me to the hospital, you'll only waste time. We don't have long.'

'What's with all the riddles?'

'Just bring me somewhere you consider safe. That's all I ask. Somewhere that is safe *for you*.'

'Phyllis locked up the station for the night. I have keys, but my superintendent might have something to say about it tomorrow. How about a coffee shop? There's one a few miles from here that might stay open.'

'What I need to say is for you only.'

'This man,' she muttered. At the same time, the phone rang.

Vicky answered, speaking low.

'Is this the right number for the Gardaí?'

The voice was deep, new; one she didn't recognise. It was also urgent.

'It is. Everything all right?'

'No, not really. There's a problem on Main Street; the waves are coming over the wall and soon they'll flood the buildings. I've tried knocking on people's doors to tell them to get out but they're either ignoring me thinking it's got to do with Halloween or like I'm messing, or something. Someone suggested calling you.'

'Hold tight and I'll come right over. I'll be there in about ten minutes.'

She hung up and turned the siren on as she sped up. 'What is it about tonight? All year round, no action, then it all comes together,' she said to herself, ignoring the passenger scowling.

Chapter 4

To Vicky, the streets of Knockfarraig were more familiar than the people, and, even in a storm were easy to navigate. Years exploring every crevice of the land aided her, for now she knew every alley, every hangout, every dodgy area and all the best streets to avoid traffic. It helped that there were barely any cars on the road this evening, the majority of residents knew well what to do when a rare storm came blowing. The parade abandoned, Vicky took comfort knowing the locals who grew up in the town would all be safe, huddled together in their kitchens or living rooms, away from the worst of it. The ones she worried about were the blow ins, the new arrivals who bought the fancy seafront houses and apartments, who'd handed over the cheque on a clear-sky day and never contemplated or saw how angry the sea could get in the winter. They had never heard the howls from the wind when sea and land collided, how it penetrated you, that sound of nature in turmoil, worse than any screeching person in pain. Every summer, the tourists' buses dropped them off and they gasped at the beauty of the place. They rarely stuck around to see the turn. To witness how vicious the sea could be. Or how unforgiving. In Knockfarraig, Vicky had watched grown women lifted off the ground when a storm hit. Or the waves surging forward, taller than mountains, an exquisite sight if it wasn't headed right towards everything you considered precious, everything you spent your life trying to protect. On a dark night when the wind and waves brought such noise it threatened to burst your eardrums, when the windows rattled and the walls appeared to tremble, it was hard to decipher its beauty when all she felt was fear. For her loved ones, for the survival of the town, for the carcass of the place that awaited when the wind calmed again.

Concentrating solely on the task at hand, it was only when she parked the car that she turned to the man. He did not look happy. She tapped at the buttons on her top.

'See this uniform? When there's an emergency, I have to help. There's no broken promise. If you sit tight here, I will come back and you can burn the ears off me for the rest of the night if your story's that long.' His arms stayed crossed. 'Or if you don't want to wait in the car, I can get someone to drive you to the hospital or I can—'

'No,' the man said. He stared out the window. 'I'll wait. Only if you'll bring me somewhere safe after? Somewhere you feel safe.'

'Fine,' she said, her mind already moved on to what she needed to do.

The sea in the distance had darkened to almost black, also, it appeared closer than normal. Along the shoreline, all you could see was white. The waves, before even breaking, still in the middle of the sea, were higher than she'd seen in her lifetime. Vicky braced herself when one hit the wall, its spray going straight up in the air, piercing the sky, then up and over like a beginner high jumper.

The storm was only getting started, the winds only testing, the waves getting angrier with each blow, yet it was already hitting the high walls and breaking them. It was only a matter of time that it would clear it without breaking against them at all. She could see it. The whole road would flood. All the businesses would be devastated, but they would survive. It was the residents that were her job, the ones trapped, or in danger. The force of the water from the next wave pushed a parked car out into the middle of the road. The unrelenting pouring rain wasn't helping matters. Or the fact she was still without a jacket.

Just as she was about to back away, a man in a red rain-jacket approached, not recognisable to her. From what she could see through the downpour, he was about her age, mid-forties, with a black beard. Another stranger tonight in a town where she knew everyone.

'Sergeant Fitzgerald?'

She nodded.

'Lenny. I made the phone call.'

She took his outstretched hand and shook. A pointless act, since both their palms were slick with rain, the skin slid past each other. The man had to shout over the sound of the waves and wind.

'We came down to help clean up after the parade, but the weather forced them to abandon it. The water broke the wall about twenty minutes ago but already it's wrecked the street. It hasn't reached most of the doors yet so some people inside aren't aware or if they are, they are afraid to answer me. It will. The worst of the storm hasn't hit; it'll get worse in a few hours. They'll lose power, could be stuck in their apartments for days.'

'You a weather expert?'

'Something like that. Can't you tell?'

Was this guy joking with her? It was too dark and rainy to see his mouth.

'A few boys from my youth group are with me. They've tried knocking on doors but people think they're messing or maybe they're freaking out and are afraid to leave their apartment. They keep shouting to stop pressing the intercom. We'll stay and help if that's okay?'

For a second, the question stunned Vicky. Used to doing things alone, her automatic response was to keep it that way. A wave crashing over the wall, landing straight on a car, forced the decision.

'Send a few lads my way. I'll knock from this end of the street; you go to the other and we'll meet in the middle. Be careful. If any waves get too close, abandon mission, yeah?'

'Sure.'

'When you knock, give it a moment, then say: "I'm acting on behalf of Sergeant Vicky Fitzgerald, we have to evacuate you immediately." Don't mention flooding or the storm, as you'll only cause more panic and you'll have a load of people scrambling out with their life's possessions. Understand?'

'Sure. I'm acting on behalf of Sergeant Vicky Fitzgerald. Got it. You got a megaphone at all?'

She tapped her backpack. 'Course I do, the best portable one you can get. Not much use over loud TVs or this wind, though. Will only add to the panic.'

'Sounds like I could do with that in the Youth Centre. You'll have to let me know where to buy one.'

Even through the pouring rain, she noticed a dimple on one side of his cheek above his beard when he smiled. Vicky never understood how anyone could trust someone based on an indentation of skin. Instead, she frowned. It wasn't exactly the time for smiling.

'Hurry.'

As he turned, she called out.

'If they parked on the street they'll all rush for their cars. It's advisable to move them, but don't suggest that until there are enough people to fill each car. People panic in these situations and get themselves hurt. Don't even mention it until we have somewhere for them to go. If there are many on foot, I'll call the local taxi company and request mini vans or something. Problem is, where are we going to take them? It needs to be big enough to hold everyone. All the local hotels are on this street.'

'We could take them to the Youth Centre. There's heating, it's on the hill so shouldn't flood. If people need to stay the night, there's enough room to lie down.'

'Youth Centre it is,' she said.

Then, without looking back, she ran to the first building on the street.

Chapter 5

The rain attacked with a collective force, slapping finger-numbing cold droplets on every inch of skin and fabric. The downpour compacted the rain close enough to appear white in the distance. It didn't fall straight down but hit sideways, accompanied by the wind, which was the genuine worry, for it contained enough power behind it to push you backwards. Her body had to fight to take a step. Trees swayed with such back and forth rhythm, it was possible to believe they were performing a Mexican wave. And the sounds; shuffling rain landing on concrete, rapping against windows. The wind had a voice that growled and whistled. The sea was another entity altogether. It howled. Screamed. The waves hitting the walls were so consuming in sound she thought her eardrums would pop. There was such beauty in this storm if you had time to stop and notice it. If you were safe indoors, wrapped in a blanket maybe. Safe indoors was a far cry from where Vicky stood now, although she wished for it with every soaking wet pore.

Lenny sent the teens over as requested, and she directed them to gather up the people they evacuated in groups in the foyer of the apartment buildings. Inside, her wind-burnt, rain-lashed skin stung and her wet clothes chafed, but she carried on. Every time they moved on to the next building, it was like re-entering a war zone; the wind blasted at them from all sides enough to turn you horizontal. In a second, the spray from the sea, gathered with the rain, soaked them right through again. Her hat was pointless. After refusing several times to just stay on her head, it had to be taken off and rammed inside her bra so she didn't lose it. Her hair, clasped together in a bun, became mostly loose, with strands hitting her eyes and face, lashing like a whip against her skin. It was too wild to fix, so Vicky pushed on. Calling each resident was a slow process, much slower than she liked. Until she gained access to the fire alarm.

'That should get their attention.'

About a third of the way through, Lenny approached.

'We have three car loads ready to go. Cal,' he pointed to one boy helping Vicky, 'will you go with them and open up, get the kettle on and get the word out to the houses around asking for a bit of milk and some spare blankets?'

Lenny dropped keys into the spotty teenager's palm.

About seventeen, the boy's eyes lit up. 'Serious, Len?'

'It's a step up in responsibility. I think you can handle it, though, do you?'

'Easy,' Cal beamed.

'Why don't you go with him?' Vicky asked Lenny.

'I can help more here. Don't worry, Cal knows the run of the place. He'll look after them until I get there. Just drive slowly, yeah?'

Cal nodded.

'Are you sure?' Vicky asked Lenny.

Although the boy had been a great help, it was too much responsibility for someone his age. Also, she knew Cal since he was a baby, knew the trouble he got into the year before, but wouldn't embarrass him by bringing it up unless she needed to. The way Cal looked at this guy was different though, around him he acted far from the aggressive boy of last year.

'I'd bet my life on it,' Lenny said.

Vicky stared at Lenny. He met her stare straight on.

'Okay,' she relented. 'Thanks for staying. And thanks, Cal,' she said, and meant it.

They worked until their clothes became like second skin, clearing everyone out. Until she was confident they'd left no one behind, mainly because you could no longer ignore the waves crashing into the street, rather than thinking it was anything to do with their evacuation. By the time they had finished, the ground floor of every building was soaking in water, despite the bags of sand placed in front.

Here's what no one tells you when land floods. The water isn't clear. Even the freshest waves from the sea turn rancid when it mixes with sewage. How can that happen? Pipes burst. Debris from leaves and twigs block drains. When the water rises, sewage rises too, until you are not wading in seawater any longer; the liquid becomes tainted with excrement, grit from roads, branches torn from trees by the wind, all joined with stones, road signs, glass. All dangers that can cut you, scrape, poison, infect.

A puddle of water pooled from her onto the floor when she sat in her car.

'You doing all right?' she asked the man. He stayed silent, and only for his eyes blinking she would assume he'd frozen to the seat.

'Look, I'm sorry, you must have thought I abandoned you. A young lad did come over like I asked?'

He gave a slight nod of his head.

'It was a long shot, trying to convince you to take a lift. I hoped you could wait somewhere warmer instead of sitting in a car getting battered by the wind. It didn't panic you, waiting all this time, not knowing how long I'd be or what the hell I was doing?'

'I knew what was going on.'

She stretched to peek out her windscreen.

'You did? You could see us?' The old man didn't move, just continued to stare out into the black. How he could see anything was the real question, but one she wasn't prepared to dive into now. There was still much to do.

'You asked for somewhere safe. Well, I found the perfect place.'

Chapter 6

When Vicky pulled up outside the youth club, the man didn't hide his disappointment. They weren't alone either; there were dozens of people getting out of cars and filing in. Rectangular in shape, with small windows dotted high on the walls and a corrugated iron roof, the youth club resembled a huge, stone shed.

'Look, I know it's not a five-star hotel, but it'll be warm and I'm sure we can find a quiet spot to talk. I'll make some phone calls while we're there, then get you home. Don't worry we don't have to stay long.'

'That's not what you promised. You said we'd talk alone.'

'Give me a break here. Can't you see I'm doing my best?' She pinched the bridge of her nose, fending off the dull ache spreading out to her temples, threatening to worsen. Sometimes, if she centred quick enough, she could stop it. She lowered her tone. 'Look, I do understand. As you can see from the uniform, even though it's soaking wet now, I am still a sergeant. Which means I have a duty to make sure all the residents of the town are safe. On any other night, my undivided attention would focus on you but tonight it's proving to be very different altogether. Will you at least tell me your name? Or else I'm going to have to call you John.'

'John?' he repeated, confused.

'John Doe.'

He held his hands out in front of him, lying them flat in the air, hovering like that for a bit, saying nothing.

'Or maybe you don't know? If that's the reason, I can help you figure it out.'

He continued to hold his hands out.

'My name is Edward.'

'Edward. Well, that's a start now, isn't it? Always better to get to know someone when you can call them by their name. Edward, how's this? We'll get everyone settled, then if we can't find an adequate area inside or you still want privacy, I'll think of somewhere. Not the station, though, it's too near the shoreline. Sound like a plan? We'll get you warmed up. I'll try to locate trousers and some shoes for you and get a towel through my hair or something and when everything calms down, we can talk.'

'Hurry,' he said.

'I'll be as quick as I can.'

Once they opened the metal door, they entered a little room that was wall to wall with corkscrew boards covered in posters advertising anti-drugs messages, support groups and details of local concerts, only breaking for a set of double doors that opened into the main room. The hall reminded her of a basketball court with no windows. The lights from the ceiling gave off a yellow hue, instantly putting Vicky in sleepy mode. Inside, the Youth Centre was a flurry of activity.

Harry O'Shea blocked her path.

'Look I think we got off to a wrong start the other week. I was wondering if we could wipe the slate clean?'

Vicky folded her arms.

'With your track record Harry, I'd need a pretty large eraser.'

Harry winced. 'So, what, nobody can change?'

'Oh, people can change, but I'm a see it to believe type of girl.'

'That's the thing though Garda, you don't even know me and you aren't letting me have a chance to show you.'

She appraised him. 'I don't see any cuffs on you.'

'True but I get the feeling that could change any second.'

'Believe me Harry, that feeling is right. You mess up at all and I'll be right on you.'

He flapped his hands to his side. 'How can anyone better themselves when people like you are just waiting for us to screw up?'

'Prove it to me and I'll be your biggest supporter.'

'What do I have to do to prove it?'

She looked around. 'Seems like there's plenty you could do around here to help. Start here.'

Harry clapped his hands together. 'Will do.'

She ignored Edward's bemused smile.

'This seat taken, girls?'

'Not yet,' Sue from the deli said, patting it while looking at Edward.

Vicky placed a hand on Margaret's shoulder. 'Look after him for a minute?'

Margaret winked. 'Course, girl.'

Vicky squatted down, so she was level with Edward. 'I'll just make sure everyone is sorted. Don't go wandering off on me, yeah?'

Edward opened his mouth as if to say something but closed it again.

Cal, the teen that helped her earlier, passed by grappling with a huge water boiler.

'Let me just check if I can get you a blanket or some trousers. See you in a second,' she said, patting Edward's hand before walking to the boy and lifting the opposite side of the boiler.

Cal's grin was huge.

'Got this from the hotel. They said they'll bring all the food over too. The water's coming right up to their reception, so all the guests are being moved here or, if they're brave enough or crazy enough to risk it, to their other hotel in the city. They may as well give the food here rather than waste it.'

'Lenny was right about you Cal; you've done a great job.'

The teen blushed bright-pink, turning his spots even redder. When he spoke, Vicky saw the flash of steel braces in his mouth. The teenage years were a tough time, poor fella. Then again, she wondered, was there any time in life that wasn't?

In tandem, they safely deposited the boiler on the nearest empty table.

Other tables lined the wall, and teens were busy filling them with items. Hotel staff placed trays of cups and plates on one. The waft of gravy and roast chicken floated over from one stacked table.

'How?' she asked.

Tony, still with his chef's hat on, shrugged. 'We were in the middle of carvery. Can't stand food waste,' he frowned. 'We had the delivery van, so stacked up all the perishables. The weather's too dangerous to drive back and forth to the city with food and they've plenty there, anyway. The hotel can claim for damages, they won't lose.'

She found Lenny unstacking chairs in a corner. Minus the red jacket, he looked different. If it hadn't been for the dimple, she would have walked past him. The hood had been misleading. With dark hair reaching his neck, long enough to tuck behind his ears, his arm muscles taut as he lifted a chair and deposited it on the ground. Tattoos peeked out from under his shirt sleeves. Grey hairs streaked through the dark hair. Men could get away with the grey, never bringing up the same connotations for women like an old hag. It suited him, gave him character.

'Thanks for letting us use this place.'

He tugged at another chair. Proving difficult to break free, she gripped the one underneath and pushed down, until the chair above came loose. Lenny grinned as he lowered it to the floor. That stupid dimple again. A droplet of water dangled from her nose. Suddenly, it mattered how dishevelled she looked. 'Anywhere a girl could freshen up around here?'

'There's a hand dryer and towels in the bathroom. Should take off some of the dampness, at least.'

'That's what I'm needing. Which way?'

'Come on, I'll show you.'

He took the hall in big strides, his long legs making it easy. She picked up the pace, catching up. Lenny was easily a head above her. As much as she didn't want to admit it, this pleased her. As she passed, Edward smiled, standing to greet her.

'Soon, Edward,' she said, ignoring his crestfallen face.

'How long have you been here?' she asked Lenny.

'At the Youth Centre or in Knockfarraig?'

'Both.'

He grinned. 'Ah, I get it. The local Garda likes to keep tabs on all her residents.'

'Exactly. I'm wondering how you slipped past my radar.'

Before he reached the double doors for the way out, he turned right towards another door, which he pushed through. This led to a set of rooms: a kitchen, what looked like an office, and two other closed doors. He stopped walking but didn't suggest where to go next.

'That's not hard since I don't live here. I'm in the city; do the commute every morning before dawn. Don't leave until it's late.' He pointed to the kitchen. 'We have a kettle, a hob and fridge so I usually have my lunch with the lads or on my tod.'

'Surely the youth club doesn't open on weekdays? Don't they have school?'

'They do. But I have a drop-in policy. I'd prefer they know they can call here rather than run off somewhere or get into trouble. Don't worry, it's above board – first thing I do is notify the school if they turn up. If they can vent, or share what's on their mind, anything that just gets the words out, then maybe I can help.'

'That's pretty noble. Now, tell me the catch.'

With a side-long glance, Lenny's smile disappeared. 'No catch. Just want to help. Here's the bathroom.'

He swung the door open, switching on the light. Surprisingly clean for a group of young teenagers and full of the type of accessories you would expect in a single woman's house rather than a youth club. In the corner, sat a basket with toilet rolls neatly lined up on top of each other, a scented candle with the wick used and free of dust, so not just for show on the shelf above, alongside a pack of wipes, sanitiser and a stack of different-coloured hand towels folded neatly next to them. There was also a shower, with a wicker table beside it, stacked high with folded bath sheets on the bottom. Vicky counted ten. From the smell, they were fresh, too. Next to it was a folded dressing gown and slippers.

'What are you running, a hotel?'

His eyebrows knitted together.

'Some of these lads need a safe place. The Gardaí aren't the only service someone can ask for help.'

'No need for the hostility, I didn't mean to offend.'

Lenny dipped his head. 'You didn't offend me, not at all.'

'Why are you frowning, then?'

Lenny closed his eyes and shook his head, then looked straight at her. 'I've never understood Cork people's obsession with sarcasm. It takes a second to unravel the twisted words, but it doesn't offend. I get why you would think there has to be a catch. In your line of work, you only see the wrong side of people. We're not all like that, though. There are some of us working our ass off to help. The youth club acts as another option. Sometimes, the people who are hurting are afraid to go to the Gardaí.'

'I know. It drives me crazy. We aren't the enemy.'

The words came out in a volley of spits. Lenny waved his hands in a calming motion.

'It's not you they're scared of. It's of what will happen if they make the call. Most of them can't foresee how it will help in the long run. All they can think about are the repercussions.' He bit his lip, stared at her. 'Right, it's me offending you now. Sorry, I'll let you dry out,' he said, stepping back.

'Lenny,' she said the word not like a name, but almost like a plea. It lingered in the air and she knew it changed something. Softened whatever it was between them. She didn't know why, but she didn't want him to go. How was that possible with someone she only knew two hours at the most?

'Yeah?' His voice barely made a sound. He stepped closer, an inch too close to class it as keeping things professional, as if he had hoped she would call him back. He parted his mouth as if he wanted to say something as much as she did, showing clean, even teeth and fleshy lips that she'd bet if she ran her tongue along would feel smooth. His breath close enough to touch her skin. She had been here many times before. Just with a different guy, in different circumstances. In a bar in the city she wouldn't pause to think, she would make a move. Revved up by alcohol, and the obscurity, she wouldn't hesitate to press her lips to his, to wrap herself around him. This was Knockfarraig, though, with her in her uniform dripping raindrops on the floor.

'Would you have any blankets to throw over Edward? Or trousers, or a spare pair of shoes even? He only has a jacket on.'

'On it.'

If this disappointed Lenny, he hid it well.

Under the dryer, she let the warm air blast, drying her damp hair and shirt. Lenny had got under her skin. When he frowned at her hotel comment, her stomach had felt like it sunk lower, like an ache down below. She was too old for childish games. Yes, the man was very attractive, but that wasn't what unbalanced her. If there was an attraction on both sides, she would have no issue exploring that; she wasn't prudish. In the past, if the urge came, if she wanted a man, she found one. Although she'd never hooked up with someone in Knockfarraig. It was too small a town to handle passing a one-night stand on the street for the rest of her life. It had been bad enough when she hooked up with Barratt, a garda at the neighbouring station, thinking she wouldn't see him again, not realising how often a station operated by one garda would need assistance. She shuddered. It was normal to feel the prickles of attraction for an attractive man, especially one who had just helped her evacuate half the town. Why did her stomach react like that, though, when he'd frowned? It wasn't sexual chemistry that made her stomach lurch. As if in warning, her body telling her not to push, not to go too far with this man. Not to hurt him. For a woman that lived off her instincts, whatever this hunch was, it was a completely new one. Lenny acted like a decent human being, but that meant nothing. The nice guy image didn't convince Vicky. That façade could easily disappear.

After her top turned from sopping to damp, she removed her boots and trousers, careful to mind dragging against the large scar on the side of her thigh. Long past healing, the scar had left the skin crepey and more delicate. She didn't like to look at it, didn't like a reminder of what happened for it to leave its mark. After squeezing the excess off the soaked cloth, she blasted the material. Only when she closed her eyes did she feel the call to sleep.

Checking her phone, there was a voice message. Selecting it, she braced herself for some other crisis. She scowled on hearing the superintendent.

'Ignoring my calls won't delay the inevitable. Avoiding my meetings won't either. No matter how much you keep burying your head, the station has to close. Despite how busy you make yourself.' He sighed into the line. 'Vicky, I get it. Knockfarraig is your home, but you're wasted there. You're always looking for trouble in a place that wants to be left in peace.' There was quiet for a moment and she thought the line would go dead, but then he spoke again. 'I wanted to tell you in person, but since I can't get you to meet or speak on the phone, you leave me no choice. They've given me a date, Vicky. The station is to close permanently on the second of November. We've sent numerous letters, but knowing you, they're probably sitting on your desk, piling up unopened. This is your official notice, Vicky. Clean out the station.

Print a sign for the front door with Ballinroe's number on it. You can report to my office on the third. I'll go through your new position then.'

Mara sighed once more.

'You're good at your job Vicky but you're reckless and dive in before you know all the facts. You know that man, Richie is suing the station? He's claiming you broke his arm. He didn't even do anything wrong.'

'Didn't do anything wrong,' she muttered.

The same guy had been prosecuted three times for rape. A complete scumbag. When she found him in his car with a young girl she had flipped. Should she have waited to hear the girl's side? Probably. But would she do it again if she thought another girl was in trouble? Over and over.

The girl wouldn't testify against him. Swore he was only helping her by giving her a lift home. Richie Collins was a scumbag, no one could convince Vicky otherwise. All she could do was hope it was proved soon to everyone else.

'I didn't even hurt him,' she said to an empty bathroom. 'He's a blatant liar, yet there Mara is asking me to trust people.'

Vicky stepped back until she felt wall. No longer a threat she could avoid, the closure was happening. The last conversation with the superintendent hadn't gone well after she had arrested a man for breaking and entering, it turned out he was the owner's nephew.

'*You never believe people. You're always looking for the crime, always looking for the negative in everyone.*'

'*That's because I always find it.*'

'*Always?*'

'*Always.*'

With the door locked, she let her eyes well. The station, *her* station, was gone. Vicky shook her hands out, trying to throw the feeling away, for she wouldn't allow a tear to shed, not here, where the red rim of her eyes would give her away.

'I'll deal with you later, superintendent. For now, I still have a job to do.'

Shoving her phone in her pocket, she dressed quickly and left the bathroom.

<h1 style="text-align:center">Chapter 7</h1>

After they fed and watered everyone, after the people who didn't have a dry home to escape to were blanketed and tucked in, after Vicky found Edward trousered in a pair of joggers and a pair of leather shoes that looked like they were at least three sizes too big, she flopped on to a chair beside him. It was only eight in the evening but felt much, much later.

'You've been very patient, Edward, thank you.'

Edward reminded Vicky of a dog she'd owned as a kid, Milo, with that faithful, eager look he used to give any time she called his name, always hoping she was ready to throw on his lead and walk him.

'Everything looks settled here. I'm sure Lenny can handle it for the rest of the night. We can find a spot to talk now if you like?'

He stood immediately, ready to go.

'Whoa there, one thing. If there are people looking for you, if there are relatives out searching in this storm, I need to know. To inform them you're safe, at least.'

He shook his head.

'Don't worry, I'll still hear you out. All I want to do is let them know. Imagine if they are out searching in this? I'll say we are just keeping you for observation for a little while and will drop you off later.'

'There's no one looking for me. I'm on my own.'

'Edward, are you sure?'

'No one's looked for me for a very long time.' His shoulders hung low at this and Vicky, even though she wanted to push more, left it alone. She would pop to the station and do a quick search as soon as the storm made it passable.

'Right then. Back there is an office and a kitchen. I could ask Lenny if we could use one room. I'm sure he'll be cool with it if I explain the situation.'

Edward rocked his head. 'No. I want to leave.'

'It's not ideal I know, but you've seen what it's like outside, it's not safe to head out anywhere and most places will shut early, anyway. We don't have many options about where to go.'

He stared at her, waiting, willing her even. The words came loose then, offering them up, involuntarily and unlike her. If she prodded at it, she would have wondered if he somehow coerced it. Definitely later she understood it as the manipulation it was, but as she said it, the words came out with such force it stunned.

'Or you could come to mine?'

For the first time, Edward smiled, his uneven yellowed teeth peeked through the crack of his mouth. He grabbed her, giving her a hug, her arms loose at her sides, not giving anything back, awkward and unwilling and a little unnerved.

Getting dry was a waste of time. Within one second of stepping out onto the pavement, the rain drenched her right through again. Cold droplets trailed down her neck. She ran ahead to the car and opened his door first. Edward shuffled along, even slower on this walk from how loose the borrowed shoes were on his feet. By the time he reached the door, his white hair was transparent, showing gaps of pink scalp. Like any other person she placed in the car, she cupped the back of his head. This time, there was a jolt, like electricity, from the rain probably, causing static or something similar. The palms of her hands felt like they were sizzling as she held the steering wheel. Not in pain, not as if burnt, but fizzing. It was as if all the nerve endings on the surface of her palms were dancing, moving around, as if the atoms and particles bumped against each other. She shook them out but gave up trying to right them. In the mirror, Edward stared back.

'I hope I know what I'm doing here,' she said.

As she drove to her house, the thought crossed her mind that she was doing the exact opposite. For a person who relied on her instinct, who always needed control, who liked rules and protocols, she was driving into the unknown.

Chapter 8

On a normal day, the journey from the youth club should have only been a five-minute drive to her door. On a night like this, it took much longer. There were many reasons for the delay: the unrelenting rain blocking her view, the car reduced to a crawling speed in order to see, the need to avoid the treacherous debris on the road. At one stage, a fallen tree made the road home unpassable, meaning a reroute and a call to the lads in the fire services.

Every eye flick in the mirror showed a fidgety Edward, looking nowhere but back at her. With no attempt at talking either, his mouth stayed in a straight line, clamped shut as if afraid to unlock his secrets too soon. After what seemed like hours, they finally reached her house.

Without a jacket, and by the time Edward clambered out of her car, there wasn't an ounce of skin dry. At her door, the water dripped down her hands in rivulets, making the key slip around in her fingers. Once it finally met the lock, she held it open wide for Edward. He didn't move.

'Go in,' she said, waving her hand to enter. The old man smiled. As he passed, a shiver ran down the length of her body. For the second time, she wondered if she had made a mistake inviting a stranger into her house. What could an old man do, though? Vicky didn't doubt her ability to look after herself. Still, this was the first time she invited anyone she met while on duty back to her house. Officially, she wasn't on duty as her shift finished hours ago, but she was still in uniform, still carrying the stance of a Garda. The superintendent wouldn't approve, but since he had already given her notice, since the station wouldn't open again, was she even still classed as a sergeant for Knockfarraig anymore? Whether she was or wasn't, sometimes being a sergeant in a rural town meant ignoring protocol.

Following behind Edward, she flicked on the hall light. Everything was just the same as she'd left earlier: the stairs directly in front running along the right side of the house, the kitchen straight ahead, with the door closed, the hall sparse except for coat hooks on the wall with the big unframed mirror, parallel to the stairs. Clean and uncluttered, just the way she liked it.

'This is where you live?' Edward asked, turning in a small circle. It was the lift in his voice that unnerved her, his surprise at where she spent her free time that made her cast an eye over the hall, trying to see it from a stranger's point of view. Every day she walked through this entrance, but it was only now, because Edward was with her, she saw how devoid of life it was, how clinical, how sparse. There was nothing of her there, no stamp, no mark, nothing that gave a glimpse of her personality, her tastes or likes. Vicky felt a flicker of shame. Purely functional, the house served its purpose as a place to lay her head at night, to sleep in after a hard shift.

'Open the door to your left and we'll get out of the cold.'

Edward did as told, and walked into the room, into the darkness. Again, Vicky flicked on the light. This room had somewhat more of her personality, hard not to as she had picked out the colours of the couch and blinds, both grey, chosen for practicality rather than preference. There were no accessories, apart from a few books stacked on top of each other on a side locker.

'No photographs?'

'I don't need to look at the dead to remember them,' she said, leaning her head on the side of the door. 'Get settled on the couch and I'll grab some towels so you can dry off.'

Upstairs, she shed her sodden clothes as quick as the stiff fabric would allow, nearly swooning at the sweet relief of feeling dry. Only comforting clothes would do on a night like this. Her softest jumper, her oldest jeans. Rooting around her wardrobe, she dragged out a black refuse bag full to the brim with Christian's clothes, intended for the charity shop. Not needing to dig too far, she pulled out an Aran-style wool jumper, a long-sleeved t-shirt and the softest tracksuit pants she could find. In her sock drawer, she picked two of her thickest pairs of fleece slipper socks and, pulling hers on, kept the other pair for Edward. Downstairs, she deposited the folded clothes beside him on the couch, along with the towels.

His skin was the colour of soured milk, dark circles ringed around his eyes. The night had not been kind to the old man.

'Are you cold? You look pale all of a sudden, Edward. If you give me a moment, I could light a fire?'

'No!'

His outburst startled her. She reached instinctively for a baton no longer there. He shuddered.

'No fire,' he said, softer. 'You only light a fire on Samhain if it is lit from the fires of Talchtga. Only then is it safe to do so.'

'Okay.' She backed out of the room. 'Oil heating then. Dry yourself off, change your clothes. By the time you're dressed, the radiators should have taken the bite off. I'll make us a drink. Tea or coffee? Or I've whiskey if you want to warm up that chest?'

Edward scooped up the clothes, leaving her question unanswered.

'Tea it is then.'

As she prepared the tea, she listened to the activity coming from the other room. At least he was doing as he was told. She yawned. Changing into comforting clothes had made her sleepy. She would give anything for an early night, slipping into her sheets and letting sleep take her.

Tempted to add a shot of whiskey to her own tea, she thought better of it, for she did not know yet what the rest of the night would bring. Despite the storm, it was still Halloween, meaning plenty of people would get drunk and messy. Active Garda or not, when the whole town knew your name and number, a phone call in the middle of the night was never a surprise. It didn't matter when her shift officially finished. If any trouble occurred in Knockfarraig, it was rarely the station's number they rang. When closed, the station's phone automatically diverted to Ballinroe which at breakneck speed was a twenty minute drive. Most of the Knockfarraig residents, the old timers at least, would never do that, always ringing her instead. In a few days, that would all be gone. What would the residents do when they needed her in the night if she was working in the city?

With the thought of phone calls, she dialled the other residential home and left a message.

Laden with tea and a tin of biscuits, Vicky placed the cup on a side table next to Edward then positioned herself in her favourite chair, a tall-backed recliner, that she sunk into rather than sat, the sides moving around her, almost cocooning. That chair was her safe place. She took a welcome sip and, for a second, relished the hot liquid warming the inside of her throat. The rain pelted the window as if tiny stones were being thrown against the glass.

'That's better. Nothing like being warm inside listening to a storm, is there? You never appreciate being indoors more than when it's lashing. So, are you happy now you've finally got me alone? Does this place meet your requirements?'

Edward warmed his hands on the tea. 'This is perfect.'

'It's like you wanted to come here all along.'

His eyes bored through her. 'That's right, I did. But I could never have suggested it. I had to be invited in.'

There was that shiver again.

Stop it, Vicky, he is just an old man.

'Edward, if I'm to take it you have been telling me the truth, you have no concussion, you haven't suffered any falls or bangs in the last few days. Dementia hasn't set in. You're completely alone in the world with no one out searching for you as we speak. You've got what you wanted, demanded even. We're now completely alone, safe, away from any threats or storms. So, unless there is any other reason, any other distraction that you can think of to again avoid my question, please finally spill your guts as to why you were standing naked in the middle of Main Street this afternoon.'

He rubbed his thighs, more in contemplation than trying to warm, she guessed. She opened her mouth to speak, thinking he was about to avoid the question, but he cut her off.

'I woke there.'

Chapter 9

Vicky put down her biscuit.

'You woke up in the middle of Main Street?'

There was no smile, no sign of him messing about. Vicky leant forward in her chair, the implications dawning.

'Hold on. Are you telling me you are a victim of an abduction? Did someone dump you there, in the street?'

He waved his hands. 'No, nothing like that. What I'm telling you is for a long moment I closed my eyes and when I opened them again, I was standing on the street. I have no explanation for why I was naked.'

Vicky pinched the bridge of her nose again, the headache brewing like the teabag she had forgotten to remove from her cup. Why hadn't she asked him about this before?

'How far away do you live?'

He stared at her with that straight-lipped look, his sign that he was unwilling to speak.

'Come on now, fair is fair. Keep to your side of the deal. You said if I took you somewhere, you would tell me. Yet here we are, I'm having to drag the conversation out of you. If you keep on withholding from me, I'll get us back in that car, storm or not, story or not, I'll dump you in the hospital and let them deal with you.'

He sighed loudly, giving in to the question. 'I don't live in Knockfarraig these days.'

'Did you drive here?'

'I'm telling you; I woke up!' The jowls under his neck shook with indignation.

Vicky tried a softer tone. 'Before today, have you ever had instances of sleepwalking?'

'Not that I know of.'

'Strange.' She opened her notebook. 'After the storm settles I can drop you home. Where exactly is your address?'

'I cannot go until I'm finished.'

She held her hands up, then looked around the room. 'What do you need to finish?'

'*How* I ended up in Knockfarraig, I don't know. But I know *why*.'

'Why?'

'I'm here for my family.'

'Only an hour ago you were telling me you had no one.'

She grabbed her phone. 'If they were expecting you, they'll be worried. Who are they? I'll ring them now.'

'You are. Victoria, you are my family. I came for you.'

Chapter 10

The phone flopped into her lap.

'Is this a joke?'

'No.'

Vicky tried to wipe away the weariness with rough swipes on her face. It didn't work.

'Everything about this night has been off. If I'd been in the station, I would have done more checks, I would have searched properly.'

I would have checked the mental health facilities.

'Don't worry, I haven't come from the asylum.'

'I'm sure you haven't. Still, I've gone about this all wrong. I've never invited a stranger into my house before. It was just that I felt a pull towards it and now, I don't know, the wrongness of it just hit me. I could get in trouble, Edward,' Vicky stood. 'Believe me, there's enough pressure on me as there is. I think we should leave.'

Edward ran his finger along the rim of the cup, the steam curling around. 'And go where? The people in the Youth Centre will have all settled now. If we go back, we will only disrupt them. The station is waterlogged, same with the nearest hotel. What is it you think I'm going to do to you?'

'How do you know the station is waterlogged?'

He screwed up his nose, confused. Straight-lipped once more. Vicky sat again, then rested her hands on the edge of the chair.

'Believe me, if I thought I was in danger, you wouldn't be sitting in my house. Try anything and you'll find that out. I'm not worried about you doing me harm. It's just protocol. I don't want to get in troub—'

'Don't worry about any trouble. Regis will be fine. Everything will work out.'

'Regis?'

'Yes.'

'Edward, I don't know any Regis.'

'Oh,' he said, confusion settled on his face. 'Who will give you trouble, then? Do you run the station alone?'

She pinched the skin between her eyebrows, trying to steer away the niggles. 'I did. I do. Apart from Phyllis, who answers the phone, I'm on my own, but I still have to answer to someone. I still have a boss.'

He tilted his head. 'You don't seem the kind to take too well to answering to someone.'

She chuckled. 'Only a few hours in my company and you can tell that already?'

He chuckled back.

'Yeah, well, that's been a problem my whole life. I do better alone and I like it that way. Advice, or more like listening to advice, are not my strongest attributes. Give me a criminal to be questioned any day, and that's where I'll shine. I'm good at asking the questions, not so much answering them.'

'Same here.'

'See now, that's where we'll butt heads 'cos you've promised me answers. We'll start with an easy one. What's your surname?'

Edward gave her a look as if that was the opposite of easy.

'Fitzgerald.'

She retraced her steps. Did she leave post lying around where he could have spotted her surname? Had someone called her by her full name earlier?

'Fitzgerald? Stop joking around. Tell me your real surname.'

'There's no joke, I promise you. I told you already I'm here for you.'

'You may think you are, but I can assure you, you're not.'

He closed his eyes for a second, then opened them wide. Smiling, he wiggled his forefinger as if inspiration hit him.

'As a child, you loved a doll with black stringed hair.'

She tilted her head, examining the man. There was no hesitation, no shake of his hands, no wild eyes or apparent signs of deliriousness.

'In fairness, I think every child owned a doll like that.'

'Her name was Crystal.'

Shit.

He smiled, more confident now.

'Your mother's name was Libbie and your father's is Brendan.'

'I don't know how you found these things out, but they aren't big secrets. With a bit of digging, anyone could discover these details.'

She didn't add that the doll's name wasn't common knowledge. That puzzle piece she would have to figure out later. Hoping the act would bring some relief from the pressure, or even a little clarity, she pinched the bridge of her nose.

'Let me get this right. You're telling me somehow you're my lost relation I've never known about, and that all of a sudden, during a storm, you decided Halloween was the best time to introduce yourself. In the middle of the street. While stripped naked?'

Edward squirmed.

'Something like that, yes. The naked thing I can't explain and I don't know all the details as such; it's not like someone has told me what to do. All I can say is that tonight was the only time I could get here. I'm here to talk, to tell you my story because I think if you listen, if you really listen, what occurred in the past may help your future.'

'Who said I need any help?'

He cocked his head. She could hear what his silence asked. *Really?*

She crossed her arms. 'I don't need anyone's help. Never have, never will.'

'Has that been working?'

'Just fine.'

'We'll see.'

'We will.'

'You like the last word, I know. If this keeps up, you'll never get to hear what I have to say. When you're ready, I can talk, but you can't interrupt until I finish. That's the deal.'

'All right. I'm ready. Work away with your story.'

'Well then. It starts with Samhain.'

Chapter 11

Physically resisting the urge to ask the man how Samhain had anything to do with her, Vicky bit down on her lip. It was hard to not ask questions. Her life revolved around discovering the solution or piecing together clues to the problem or being haunted by the unanswered ones.

'Samhain isn't about treats or costumes, or how much you can scare. It represents the start of a new year, when autumn turns to winter, celebrated from when the sun goes down on October 31st till the sun sets on November 1st. Samhain is an Irish tradition, originates long before St Patrick's day, running longer than Christmas even, before Catholicism landed in Ireland. They changed it, the Catholics, changed November 1st to All Saints' Day, changed Samhain to All Hallows Eve, which turned into this Halloween lark. They wanted to eradicate any ritual that wasn't Catholic in nature, calling it evil. In doing so, they erased our ways, erased our reasons for the celebration. It was the time of Tara and Fionn MacCumhail and Cuchulainn. Of Donn, the Lord of the Dead. Do you know the story of Samhain, how it originated?'

'The bones of it, what they taught in school.'

The wind interrupted their conversation with a tree branch knocking against the window. Not that the wind had eased, still in vicious form, every couple of seconds it gathered momentum and raged. Random noises cut through the silence; the scraping of a soda can, the clatter of a plastic lid, the thump and scrape which she could only imagine was the knocking over of a bin. The trees outside her house rocked from side to side until they were almost horizontal. Not a night to venture outside. A screech sounded like a kettle staying on the boil, scratching at the ears, piercing the drum. There was a constant shooing, similar to the sound when you cover your ear with a shell, but this noise didn't bring you to the sea, rather to its opposite, to the air, whirling and demonic in the sky.

She settled back into the chair, trying to relax, reminding herself to appreciate the dry and warmth. But something else mingled with the appreciation, for she was also a little afraid of what this man may say to her.

'Over the course of Samhain, I will tell you three stories. In this one, the first one, there is also three. They are linked, although you may not understand why for a while. Listen. It is important you listen; there is a lot to learn from these things. And although what I say may suspend belief, I want you to trust me enough not to dismiss it. I know for you, that will be hard.'

'Course I can listen. In my job you have to be good at listening, and Edward, despite what you think you know, I'm good at my job.'

Edward bowed his head, acknowledging her words. He straightened, sat back in the chair. 'Then we can start.'

Chapter 12

'Three stories. One is mine, one is about someone dear to me, one is about someone dear to you. At the moment, you are apprehensive, but soon you won't be, for you will find yourself sucked in and may even find, by the time I finish, you want more answers. I will give you all I have, nothing more. There will be interruptions, I promise you that, for I cannot control the makers at play. You might hope to delay it also, but there is a time limit here. For me, I am limited, my opportunity will soon run out. You could argue all our days are limited and that is the truth. For me though, it is hours. Who knows for you? It's the Russian roulette of life, we take the gamble, we have no choice but to take the gamble. If we are lucky, we're awarded safe passage through a long life. Every life is temporary. We are all scraping borrowed days. Tonight though, there will be no hurry, for Samhain is the night to let visitors talk. It is the time for stories and if the hour goes too quickly, the spirits have a way to slow the world down.'

'Are we going down the road of spirits, Edward? Because I'll tell you right now I don't believe, and I don't want no part in that type of talk. I can't stand the old ghost stories and there hasn't been one thing in my whole life to convince me any of that is true.'

Edward cocked his head. 'You don't believe in good and evil?'

'Evil, I believe in. I have seen many examples of pure and utter evil. But that is always man-made. Manufactured by a living being. What I don't believe in is dark spirits, of lingering omens or curses. They wrote those Irish traditions to keep the people in check; to keep them in fear so they wouldn't step out of line. We make our own luck in life. People become or learn to be evil.'

'Do you believe goodness is man-made, too?'

She shrugged. 'I guess. Good intentions often ruin goodness. We are our own worst enemies; man ruins every good thing.'

'Like?'

'Love. Friendship.'

Edward folded his arms and smiled. 'How is love ruined?'

'Jealousy. The need to control. The need for power. Betrayal, lies, wanting to keep the person from changing. Have I listed enough?'

He regarded her and tilted his head again. 'Yes. You have said enough.'

'My job sees more activity from love gone wrong than plain evil.'

Edward stayed silent.

'Sorry, you have a way of making me want to speak. No more interruptions. I'll only speak if you want me to.'

'I will start with the story about a person dear to me. Are you ready?'

He rolled his hand towards her as he asked the question. Leaving the ball in her court, giving her a chance to refuse.

Without a beat, she answered, 'yes.'

It was only after she wondered if she should have hesitated, for there was something in the way he asked, some threat hidden in the question that made her wonder if she wanted to hear, or if she was ready for what he had to say. Vicky was not one to pay heed to her fears, she was always one who would carry on, regardless. Yet, it was only when Edward spoke again did she release a breath. His voice melodic and used to storytelling, he carried her off into the story until she forgot her fears.

For a moment, at least.

Chapter 13

'There is a place buried deep in the woods. A hidden place, not easy to reach, full of brambles and thorns, bushes and nettles, and, although it is treacherous, all who have been there have considered it worth the trek. Through the years, some have believed the place to be magical, some have said it is cursed, but I'll let you make up your mind about that. For the most part, on most days, it is a tranquil clearing hidden behind trees and facing a river. Throughout history, numerous stories have unfolded on that very spot. Amongst them, a battle, a marriage, and copious deaths. Mostly, though, it is a place of reflection, a place where time can still and people can sit and ponder.

'On the 31st October 1900, there is a girl under the tree, her long blonde hair swept to one side, draping down over her shoulder and settling on her stomach. Her blouse is well worn, tattered, you could say. The shawl wrapped around her hides the worst of the mended rips and prevents the breeze from cutting into her skin. Stains cover the front of her apron, for in her haste to leave she never thought to remove it. The long skirt flares out as she sits. She senses she is on the cusp of womanhood, proven by the changes in her body: the swell of her breasts, the dip in her waist, the broadening of her hips, the difference in the shard of mirror reflecting her pronounced lips and the rise of her cheekbones. More so, she has noticed the change in attitude from the men in the village, with their side glances and the way some follow as she goes about her business.

Some have been blatant, telling her she is the finest girl they have ever laid eyes on and this she believes, not through any care for her looks herself but because the women in the village act differently around her too of late, going silent when she stands in line at the well, some crossing their arms and turning their backs even though there hasn't been one cross word said between them. If they did speak, she would tell them she has no mind for proposals, for she has only just turned fifteen and is not ready for betrothal. She knows nothing about the ways of marriage yet can still understand why the single women turn their back, some of them ten years older and afraid of being labelled spinsters, yet here she is with not one but two proposals made, both she wants no part of, even though it has become apparent she has no say. *That* choice won't be hers. Her mammy and daddy haven't even told her, have given no inclination, only that she overheard the men, as they called to the door, and although she didn't see the first one, she could picture him as he spoke, his voice gravelly and old, much, much older, and she shuddered and tried to shiver the thought away. Her initial reaction was to run out from the kitchen, and shoo the man away, telling him her family would have no part in it, but when the talk turned to what he could offer and her mammy and daddy didn't stop the conversation, just let him continue, she froze to the spot.

'Times were difficult and with more mouths to feed now that Mammy's tummy was getting big again and with nine other smallies all born barely over a year apart and her being the eldest, there was pressure to bring more money in. At first, she didn't understand the word the man said, didn't know this word dowry, that he kept drawing out, sounding long, coming out of his mouth like he was speaking about a prize. Until he said, 'Sir, I would gladly refuse any dowry for her to be my bride. In fact, I would give you one.'

'Then she understood, she was being bartered for, sold on, like a cow at the market.

'A week later, today, at around the same time as the last visitor, they banished her outside to hang sheets on the line. When she heard the rusty gate creak open, this time she cottoned on her parents hadn't wanted her to be inside the house. As the sheets billowed and flapped, she stole a peek through a gap, and baulked on seeing the man, wishing she had kept her eyes on her task. At a guess, the man making his way to the door was no younger than forty at least, fifty even, with a full straggly beard and unkempt appearance. Somehow, the town had decided she had come of age. Dumping the laundry on the ground, without another thought, she had ran. Ran and ran, straight to this spot, her secret hiding place, to sit and contemplate her future.

'And this is where we find her, under the tree, trying to decide her own fate.

'Her family were poor, and each day was a struggle to claw enough from any means. If she loved them, surely she could make this sacrifice? Could she leave her whole family and live with a stranger? She knew nothing of marital expectations, except sometimes she heard moans late at night coming from behind the hung sheet on the other side of the room. If she was honest, the sounds sent a chill up her back. Was that to be expected? Was that every woman's fate? Her mother often sounded like she was groaning in pain. When she heard the motion, the banging or creaks from the bed, she would cover her ears and swear she wanted no part in it, no part at all. Yet her parents always went about their day with a gentle love, with never a harsh word spoken between them. Which made the change at night even more confusing.

'She loved her mammy and her daddy, and her brothers and sisters brought much joy to her life, but they had all felt the hunger this last winter when the crops had taken a blight, reminding them of the great famine, a time she was old enough to remember and lucky enough to survive. Her bones had only just started filling out. Last year reminded them all too well of the hunger they had once felt. She had been born into the famine, her whole life surrounded by starvation and the hunt for more food. No one could go back to that. If her parents needed to sacrifice their oldest child to a loveless marriage, they would do it if it meant none of their family would starve. She remembered the hunger, the pain of not eating, how the stomach could physically spasm for food, making her bend over with wanting. Starvation is an agonizing way to die. Her parents were never the same after Seamus, once the oldest child, her brother, died on the side of the road, one minute alive and talking and then just keeled over, straight down, his heart just giving out. They would never forget that. They would do anything to stop that from happening again. What was their daughter marrying a village man compared to feeding eleven mouths? Thirteen if you counted hers and the new baby in her mammy's stomach. She was sure her parents would weigh up the choice, do their homework, pick the best of the lot, but what about love?

'She had always dreamed of a love match. Of meeting her husband, seeing him one day as they both went about their business, and that her heart would know before her head, jolted as if electrocuted, where life as she knew it would never be again. It wasn't like she had romantic notions, or dreamt of a man whisking her away, and she surely didn't want to be saved as it was. When she had pictured growing older, she had imagined a great love story, a partner to share her life with, a friend to grow old and rear children together because she had witnessed long enough how hard existing could be. Being with a person you liked softened the harshness of what it threw towards you. There were always rumours of wives who didn't have it so lucky. She heard the violent words passing between couples on the road. Or the women who had to walk behind their husband, only speaking once spoken to, who had no say at all in matters of the family. Her father, behind closed doors anyway, always let the women speak freely. It worried her now if she had no choice in who to pick for a husband, if her parents would even consider these things. No matter how she reasoned, the thought of leaving her family and living with a man, a stranger, left her nauseous. Because even if he was kind, and soft hearted and not a brute, she would spend the rest of her life fetching for him, her fate sealed to nothing more than the life her mother had; a life of rearing children, of being pregnant or with a child constantly on a hip or breast. There was nothing wrong with that type of life as such, but it was just not what she had pictured when she had dreamt of getting older. It was not something she felt ready for.

'Instigated by fear, her thoughts went in another direction, towards another option she would never dare to have admitted to dreaming of before. Dangling between a decision that would keep her innocent, or at least innocent to the world of a husband, or accepting the fate of her parents' choice. Either way, however she looked at it, after this day, her life as it was once, was over. The decision she would make would certainly propel her into a new life, but what that life was to be, she was unsure.

'We never understand that this world has been here longer than our existence. Each rock. The soil. The sky. All ancient amongst us. Even adults are nature's children.

'If only she knew where she was sitting. If only she knew she was sitting on the throne of unknown legends. Of heroes who died not raising a fuss. Who didn't speak loud enough or long enough to have books written about them but still meant everything to the people who lived on. Until they too died. Time leads to everything becoming forgotten, eventually. That place, that tree, never forgets. Each person, every visit etched into the wood, their fragrance mingled with the flowers, their dust blown with the breeze.

'Looking to the river, the water reminded her of the boats she spotted on her last visit to Queenstown, where she waved back to the people on the ship as they left the dock in the early morning. She had asked a man if they recognised the flag on the ship, if they knew why those people were leaving and the dock worker had sparked up a rollie.

"They're the lucky ones, swanning off to make their fortune. To the land of the free called America. Fields covered with gold there, they say."

'In a crowd of brown and grey clothed people, she caught sight of a woman dressed in pale-blue, standing alone, as if the others surrounding her had set such a finely dressed lady apart. A large cream hat sat on her head with a long blue sash. The material caught the breeze, flapping its full length into the air, dancing with the wind. The woman didn't appear frightened or resigned. From across the dock, her smile, her pride, her excitement, was clear. In that moment, she wished she could replace her, be the one standing on that ship, looking back at the dock. What would that woman see in her? A raggedy girl with nothing in her pockets staring back.

'Ever since that day, as she went about her chores, she had dreamt of the place called The Land of The Free, where they allowed women to make their own choices, where the possibility of freedom existed, where wives didn't have to toil all day, cleaning and cooking and raising children. What would freedom feel like? Could she even do it? Could she run away, leave her family behind, go to America and start a new life? If she was brave enough, she would have to do it soon, as every hour she lingered, her mind changed. Hesitation rots bravery. It rots courage and gumption until it only leaves behind a soft shell of what could have been. Was she a good girl? What lay for her if she did what her family needed? Yes, it would break her family's heart to run, but what of it if the choice was for her heart to break instead?

'The day she saw the woman in the blue dress, she pushed past the crowd of market hagglers, followed along until the dock end and stayed there until the ship disappeared on the horizon. As she was leaving, a man handed her a leaflet saying *Steam to New York once a week.* The steerage was five pounds. A sum she had no chance of coming up with for that was over half the family's earnings for a year. But what if she snuck on? What if she promised to marry a man from the town, then ran away with the dowry? Yes, her decision would vex her parents, crack their hearts in two. When she started sending money home, though, they would be happy. Surely, once they understood her plans, they would forgive her. Could she live the life she wanted and give them what they needed too? Was she brave enough to try?

'If you visit those woods, touch the bark of the tree, you will find it smoothed on the underside from years of people using it as back support. You might wonder who has lain there unknowing the girl was one of them, or the decision she agonised over, deciding her fate against that very tree.'

Chapter 14

Edward stopped for a second and gulped, as if speaking that much winded him. This time Vicky didn't break the silence with her questions, even if it was a conscientious one to offer him water. Instead, she pondered her own. Had she ever stopped and wondered about the people who trudged steps on the same ground before her? Or of the history of each place. Of the happiness, of the memories of people long gone. Could a feeling stay? Did the weight of decisions settle in the air around a person, mingle with the earth, etch into the surrounding nature? Was a memorable event remembered by the birds and animals, by the trees?

Edward spoke again, breaking her question trail.

'As a child the woods are a place to play, a place to run, chase, explore. As a man, I view it as a place of history. A reminder of our insignificance. Each adult tree is older than any of us. Most will outlive a child born this very day. We should bask in their glory, thank them for not only their conversion of air, making it possible for us to breathe, but for their shelter, for the peace they've already given. When we are all long gone back to the ground, the woods will live on. What will it see?'

Vicky didn't interrupt with an answer, knowing whatever she could say was pointless. There wasn't one correct response anyway, only a list of multiple options, all only guesses, only speculative. She just wanted Edward to carry on, to tell her of this girl, of what was to become of her. Even though she was a stranger, she wanted the outcome.

'In this place, hidden deep inside the woods, there is a large clearing that opens out onto a field full of bluebells in the summer. Even in the winter, when the ground frosts over and no flower survives, the sight of the immense tree overlooking the river is still as breathtaking. There is a stillness there, a stillness that some search for, while it only torments others. The place doesn't cause their anguish, rather the silence does, and when a person catches themselves in the river's reflection, it acts like a mirror, showing them what they've tried to hide from everyone, including themselves. The place shows their truth, revealing what they really contain inside.

'On this day, the wind hadn't picked up yet, the plants and flowers on the other side of the water stood tall and unmoving. The river made sounds, but it was peaceful. The sound of liquid making its way over stone and pebble, because no journey, even an easy one, stays smooth. Yet, it was unstoppable. No matter how highly stacked the stones, or how deep the rivets dug and seemed certain to block the path, the water always overcame. As clear as glass, the water was inviting on that last summer's day. He would not drink it, though. Instead, he splashed the water on his face, sat back with his skin to the sun and waited for it to dry. He enjoyed feeling the drips roll down his neck. It brought him back to the present, and he wanted to remember every second of this day. As he waited, he was grateful for the sounds of the river, grateful that it blocked the noise coming from his beating heart.'

'Wait,' Vicky said. 'Are you not going to tell me what happened to the girl? Are we finished with that one and on to the next?'

Edward didn't look impressed with the interruption. 'By the time I am finished, the details will make sense. Remember? Trust me.'

'Fine,' she said, and settled in the chair. The clock on the wall had stopped ticking. Vicky checked her watch and stared until she gave up, the turning of the minute way longer than normal. Many times before, she heard of time slowing on Samhain. In the tales of the old folklore, in the ghost stories that kept her up way longer than just on Halloween night. She pushed the thoughts away once Edward started his tale again.

'When he heard the rustling grass, he thought he would die from the shivers of joy that ran through him, because until that moment, the fear had clung that she wouldn't show, that she had changed her mind and decided not to, and even though he had yet to see if it was her, just from the sound of feet on grass, a delicate step as if parting the blades rather than bashing them into the ground, it convinced him it was her. Because even though they could only have a few minutes each day to talk, only ever have enough time to catch glimpses, stealing lingering looks when no one else was paying attention, it was as if he knew every part of her, knew every gesture and trait. He longed to touch her jawline the next time she turned shy and dipped her head. He yearned, ached, to trace his fingertips along those long eyelashes.

'Even expecting her arrival, his mouth gaped when he saw her, his first thought being that he had never seen such a sight, and he said a silent prayer to above that if this was the last vision he ever saw, or if he indeed was already dead and this was only an apparition, he would gladly feast his eyes on it for all eternity. With wildflowers weaved in her hair and dressed in what should have been her wedding dress to another man, it was him she moved towards. The rest of her hair hung loose and fell to her hips. He had never seen her hair free before, framing that beauty. It took any words from him. How many months had he resisted taking her bun and unpinning the hair trapped inside, so he could run his fingers through? On seeing him she smiled, and trailed her hands over the bluebells, picking at some until she had a bouquet of at least a dozen, holding them in front of her as she walked towards him on her solo wedding march.

"Never a more beautiful bride did a woman make."

"Never a handsomer husband."

"Your smile, Deirdre, would turn any winter to summer."

'They were nervous when they reached each other, but as his hands touched hers just once, he knew whatever repercussions were to come of this it would still be worth it.

'He took the piece of twine he had searched high and low for and showed it open palmed.

"Are you sure?"

'Her face, solemn at first, broke out in a huge grin, and it was her turn to hold out her hand. Inside one palm was a folded hanky, which she unfolded now to show two wedding rings.

"I'm sorry your friends can't be here, or your family."

'She tilted her chin, showing that defiance he loved.

"What of it? They will give us their blessing once it is done. They will celebrate with us when it is law."

'That time she had come to the woods; she had wronged her parents. They would rather starve than see her married to an unworthy man. She did the right thing.'

'Yes!' Vicky said. Then, 'Sorry.'

Edward gave her a warning grimace, then carried on.

'Instead of keeping secrets, that day I spoke about earlier, when she arrived home, she told her parents of her plan, suggesting they all set sail on a boat to America or she could go alone with the dowry and send money home. There was no need, they said, to marry a man she couldn't bear. They had survived worse before and would again. Enough vegetables in the garden meant they wouldn't starve, and wasn't she old enough to work and help? That was worth more to them than any dowry.

'As the fear left, her beauty only blossomed more. Word got out around the town that if some man planned a proposition, they were to call on a Monday on washing day, as Deirdre would be busy in the garden putting out the line. After that, every Monday morning, a new caller would chance a proposal. Sometimes there was more than one, lined up along the lane, young and old. Some travelled quite a distance, after seeing her in the market in the next town or hearing of this great beauty from a passing rebuked traveller. On each occasion, after they made it clear the intention of the visit was to ask for her hand, one of her parents made an excuse to go to the kitchen to seek their daughter's opinion. There was always a shake of her head. As soon as she'd given them the sign, they wrapped it up and sent them on their way.

'Until, that is, the British officer Willmott spotted her in town. A spindly, sharp featured man who Deirdre would rather take her chances to swim to America and drown than spend a minute in his company. Willmott proved different from the other respectful suitors when her parents declined his advances. Used to a lifetime of getting his way, Willmott declared in front of a crowd after their polite refusal that no one in the town would marry Deirdre except him. Every day after, some package arrived: bouquets of flowers, bread, the finest cuts of meat wrapped in paper, even once a ring. Deciding the soft approach from her parents wasn't working, Deirdre took matters into her own hands. She stomped to the barracks and demanded he take back the ring, but he refused to take possession of the box. Frantic, she placed the box by his feet and yelled at him then that she may be poor, but Éire still allowed her freedom of choice, and she didn't want him, or his ring, and would never marry him. It didn't matter what she said. He just laughed and called her foolish, saying he loved that about her, her spirit, and he would spend a lifetime of their marriage convincing her of his love. The next day's package was once again the ring.

'When the wedding gown arrived, her breath reduced to shallow gasps for days. When he sent an invitation to her for her own wedding, the walls building up around her took on a roof. Willmott's message was clear: he was taking her as a bride. No wasn't an answer. He would carry on regardless, with her permission or without it. The wedding date he chose was her next birthday, nearly a year away. Officer or not, there were still some laws he had to abide to and as her parents had refused consent, Willmott was forced to wait until she turned seventeen.

'And then her life changed. As old man Roche's horse collapsed in the middle of the street right in front of her, a young man cleaning himself in the stream rushed over to check on the animal. When nothing could save the mare, after the man soothed the horse's passage to death with his gentle whispers, he called on the men standing around to help. Deirdre watched as he picked up the horse's leg and moved the animal, his instructions clear and his voice commanding enough that each man pulling fell in step. He guided the men to lay the animal down on the side of the road. Deirdre took in his ragged clothes, the sole coming away from one of his boots, the welts on his knuckles, and saw nothing that she minded.

'Before the man even noticed her, before their eyes locked, the thought came to Deirdre that he was the exact type of man she had refused all others for. A man who displayed kindness when he wasn't aware who was watching. With obvious morals. Who could move carts with his hands, who could shift other men to do it too. After their eyes locked, she knew with a certainty, that the man she would marry would be him.

'For him, it was instant, too. As he laid eyes on her, he flustered, dipping the cart. Until the man beside him grunted and lurched forward, about to drop his hold. Only then did he drag his gaze away, righting himself, he moved the cart from the middle of the road, laying it beside the dead mare.

'When he looked away, it felt like night descended. Never before had her senses danced. Deirdre felt fire in her stomach, lightning in her head, cold running through her blood. For he was finally there. The man she had waited for, the man she had refused all others, in the hope, in faith that the one she felt she already knew was making his way to her.

'She only broke her gaze when Beatrice nudged her in the ribs.

'As they left to find a method to take away the horse, with the old man Roche crying like he had lost a child, he stole another glance, then tipped his head at her. A gesture she would hold on to, would cherish for weeks. Deirdre whispered to Beatrice, the closest she had to calling a friend, "Who was that?"

"That's the Fenian."

"Fenian?"

"Jesus, Deirdre, you should start listening to the talk in the village. He's with the brotherhood?"

'She rolled her eyes at Deirdre's confusion. "The IRB, the Irish republican brotherhood. They say he served time with Clarke in England a few years ago. He's already been causing a stir with Willmott."

'That alone was another reason to love him.

'After that day, she made it her business to seek him out. It wasn't hard. In a small town, where anything different goes noticed, whispers flurry everywhere. Sleeping in a tent with three others, they were travelling the country to spread Clarke's words of bravery, and of freedom. Once she gained the knowledge of the general area he resided, she made it her business to find a task to take her nearby. On second sight, she loved him more. His darkness was the opposite to her light features. His dark-brown hair flopped around his face. When he smiled, he revealed a longer than average eye-tooth, pointed to a razor-sharp edge, which instead of making him appear harsh, gave him a roguish appearance, only adding to his value in her eyes. When he saw her, he again dropped what was in his hands. This time it wasn't a cart but a cup. This time he acted on his impulses. He strode out and met her in the middle of the street. They stood in front of each other for an exquisite time. Deirdre had never wanted to touch a stranger before. She had never wanted to touch anyone before. In that moment, she understood what it meant to want to live. All the days toiling, of suffering, all the days ending dreary and dark were her only paying her dues to be afforded this, for right in that moment she understood. The feelings stirred inside her were the sole purpose in living. All her days had built to this. Before, she lived without knowing what this could feel like, only guessing, only hoping, with a faith she didn't understand, just a knowing, deep inside, to wait, that if she did, one day her reward would arrive. Now she understood what she had lived before had only been a half-life, an uncompleted existence, for his gaze upon her, his want, his interest, had awakened what it really felt like to live. Every refusal, every shake of her head, every man she had sent away, was rectified. For nothing could compare with how one pointy tooth could spark a lightning bolt. No words could justify the feeling. Deirdre knew this was the greatest of love stories and it was hers and his and could not be tainted or touched by any other but the two of them.

'She found an excuse to pass that resting place at least once a day, and no matter what he was doing, he fell in line with her stride. There were words between them, where he told her of his time with Tom Clarke, how the man had ignited in him a bravery that he never thought he was capable of. He had sworn to the man he wouldn't rest until they had a free Éire again. Deirdre spoke of the daily toil from working on the land, with never enough to feed her family. She offered to sew up his rags and brought hay to line his boots so his feet would no longer touch the dirt. It was hidden inside the words they didn't say, that confirmed their true feelings. When it was time to say goodbye yet neither of them made the move to leave, the many times they looked back when their tasks tore them away from each other and they had to leave, when silently, both of them would count the minutes, feeling like they were holding their breath, until the next time. And then, when he should have been moving on, when he should have been travelling to the next town, Brendan paid her family a visit and stood outside the house on a Monday, knowing already deep in his heart, the answer to his question would be very different, knowing already her answer would be yes.'

He has the same name as my father, Vicky thought.

'Deirdre's family only had to meet Brendan once to know, without even getting the nod from their daughter, that he was the one. Believing in the sanctity of marriage, they convinced the couple not to run, that once they took their vows, it would force Wilmott to respect the law. Brendan disagreed, witnessing many a sergeant kill for much less than a beauty like his soon-to-be wife. They hatched a plan, a secret plan, so Willmott wouldn't hear, wouldn't try to arrest him or force him out, or kill him. Brendan opened a business as a tobacconist with the support of Clarke in a nearby village.

'Before their ceremony, Brendan turned to Deirdre.

"What about Willmott?"

"I have told him I love another."

"And he accepted that?"

'She shook her head. "I told him that one day, he will see we were not suited, that another will love him more than I. That he is a good man and will find a woman perfect for him, like I have found the one for me."

'He stroked her hair, each strand glistening as if spun through with threads of gold.

"There is nothing I can offer you, Deirdre, but I swear, no man has ever loved another as much. To prove my love, I am willing to let you go. If you marry him, you will never want for anything, he will give you everything you desire: food and gold and security. I can offer you no such thing, for a Fenian works for Éire and serves her land. Even before he hears of our marriage, you know Willmott saw me as the enemy? You want to see the good in him, but there's only rottenness there, and we will expose the rot when he doesn't get what he wants. He will kill me without a second thought, but if he tries to hurt you, I can't bear it. Your life will be at risk. We will have to leave. It isn't fair to expect you to leave your loved ones for me."

'Deirdre placed a finger to his lips. "What I desire is love. I would rather die after a day with you than live a lifetime with him."

'Once wed, they would leave the next day, onwards to the next town to spread Clarke's word. If he could, he would have married her far away from Knockfarraig, but to travel with an unmarried woman without a chaperone, even if it was only to their wedding, may have scared away a priest who didn't know their circumstances. Putting aside his fears and worry, for loving Deirdre meant more, they set the secret wedding.'

Chapter 15

'In hushed tones, they spoke their vows in front of the priest, in the same place Deirdre had sat a year and a half before, trying to decide. As the sun set, and the sky turned everything pink, as the tree branches swayed in celebration, and the water glistened with what appeared like pink crystals on the surface, they slipped bronze bands on each other's fingers. Then the priest tied their hands together and, with his blessing, pronounced them man and wife. They didn't move until after the priest had rushed off and only then, it was to lie on the ground under the tree, where Brendan spread flat a blanket he'd brought, and covered another over them, then ate a feast of cheese and bread. Under that sacred tree, they shared their first kiss, their first everything. On their wedding night, the stars became their lamps and the grass their bed, each other's arms their blanket. Every person deserves a night like that; a night they are the happiest they will be.

'By the next morning, they were no longer two but three. Not knowing how little time they would have together, how an ambush was waiting for them all night, the men laughing and sniggering at the couple's naivety, at their wrong perception of privacy. By nightfall Brendan would be dead, his last sight Willmott's knife, held down by two men on either side, leaving Deirdre a widow. Those same disgusting men would walk into town led by a grinning Willmott, singing of how they had caught the great Fenian, a rebel no more, all the while covered in his blood, singing their

English songs, denouncing the wedding and the God of their enemies, unaware of the baby already incubating in the new mother's belly, for, if they had any inkling, they would surely have put a knife in her stomach and ripped his descendant out. For now, was an heir to all that they despised. Through grief and sorrow, a son of a Fenian would grow.

'He did not touch her, at least. After Willmott made her watch her husband die, he spat on the wilted wildflowers in her hair, saying he would never touch a soiled woman.

'Before the Irish Volunteers and the Easter Rising, before the execution of his mentor Tom Clarke by firing squad in 1916, before the burning of Cork in 1920 which saw the buildings of Patrick Street burned to the ground and turned to rubble by the British Army. Before all this, when Britannia ruled Ireland, an army officer saw nothing at all in erasing a love rival from the earth.

'Her family, hanging their heads as the men passed, said nothing, even though they knew whose blood soaked their clothes. Inside, their hearts broke. The whole of Knockfarraig knew of the secret the couple had tried to hide, because you cannot conceal pure love. It is evident to anyone who lays witness. After the soldiers passed, they ran to the woods searching for the screaming bride, ripping their skin on thorns and stinging nettles. They could not get lost, for all they had to do was follow the screams, the caoineadh of a woman who knows her great love has been ripped away. And when they reached her, Deirdre looked half dead herself, her pale skin and Willmott's wedding dress dyed crimson with blood, laying across her dead husband. The bluebell bouquet lay limp beside his new shoes given to him the week before as a wedding gift from Deirdre. His blood pooled around his lifeless corpse, black and oozing like melted liquorice. It seeped into the ground, trailing a line to the river. His blood mixed with the soil, flowing down until it fertilized seeds previously parched, giving them enough life to bear flowers, enriching the tree's roots and embedding his cells into the wood's memory.

'Only once they promised to return to bury her husband did she allow them to pry her fingers away from his body and carry her to her house. In the same spot he turned from bachelor to husband, from living to dead and where she turned from virgin to mother, they held a funeral for Brendan.

'On more than one occasion, her mother had to wrestle a knife from Deirdre's hands on her way to the barracks in search of Willmott. Wild in her grief, there wasn't anything a person could do to help. Each day, she returned to the place by the tree. On her journey, the whole town heard her caoineadh, her lament, over and over. Until her breasts swelled and her stomach grew, when a new love and sense of purpose blossomed inside of Deirdre. For now she understood she had kept a part of Brendan and carried evidence that the brief love they shared existed, in spite of Willmott doing everything to destroy it. The day she discovered her pregnancy, she moved away; to hide until the child was born and she could announce his rightful place.'

Chapter 16

'That was the end of the second part of the first story.'

Vicky sat back, settling her nerves.

'Can I ask a question now?'

He smiled, bent his head. 'That you can.'

'What happened to Willmott?'

'On first hearing, his ending wasn't what you would imagine. He died alone in a ditch, after falling while relieving himself after a night drinking.'

'In Knockfarraig?'

'Yes.'

'How long after?'

'A year to the day Brendan died.'

Vicky tsked. 'What a coincidence.'

'Coincidence, yes, people believed. Many soldiers argued that the blood covered rock Willmott fell on was too far away from where his body lay and also at the wrong angle for his head injury. No matter how much they protested, how many rumours they spread about Clarke's vengeance, there were no arrests made. Nobody ever proved a thing. They didn't even bring in any suspect for questioning, for not one soul mourned the loss of the man. No one discovered the truth, either. And even if they did, even if someone from the town had eyed her hiding in the woods waiting, or witnessed his murder, they wouldn't have told anyway.'

'Was Deirdre all right, after?'

'She lived, Victoria. She found a way to live.'

'Good for you, Deirdre,' she said, only loud enough for herself to hear.

'You ready for the next part?'

'There's more?'

'Much.'

Chapter 17

'In 1941, a man stood by the same river, flicking stones and skimming them across the surface. With a heavy heart, he waited. Many times he visited this place. In his childhood years, he and three others made a swing and used the tree's heavy branch to leap from the ground and hurl over the water. In his teenage years, he led his sweetheart Mary by the hand and showed her the place his mother married his father and the tuft of ground where his father died, and his own life began.'

Vicky clapped her hands together, startling Edward. 'Sorry, don't stop, I just wondered what happened to the child, that's all.'

'Where once a small cross stood; the only sign of where his father died. Since hearing of the importance of the land to his family, he since had added his own history; proposing to Mary after the long apprenticeship with the old man McDermott, when he could finally believe he was worth marrying. It was where he had returned and dug out the cross and with a block of marble carved and etched his father's name and history, naming himself as his descendent. Then, years later, with a heavy and broken heart, he etched his mother's name and date of death underneath. In this same place, he waited for Mary now, for a picnic with their two little ones. In the exact place a fresh blanket lay thirty-nine years before, he smoothed out his own.

'When she arrived, holding hands with both their children, he imagined his mother making this same trek on the day of her wedding. Mary was beautiful. Different to his mother, for beauty has many shades and for his mother's blonde, Mary's hair was as black as coal, her dark eyes the only darkness he ever witnessed in the nineteen years he'd known her, five in marriage. His two children inherited her dark hair and eyes, and he often gasped at the sight of them. Now, he took in that beauty as if it would be for the last time, because he knew, after this day, after he informed her he had signed up, he would not see that smile again. Not knowing he would never.

'After the children had eaten and ran into the field with the new ball he gifted them, when he and his wife had a quiet moment cut through with occasional whoops of joy from his son and daughter, the man chose his moment to rip apart his family.

"Tell me what you've done. The only reason you've brought me to my favourite place is to soften me up."

"You could take a job as a mind reader, Mary; you would make a fortune."

"Only problem is, you're the only person I've ever been able to read completely."

"This time it mustn't have worked, because if you could read my mind now, you wouldn't be smiling."

'Her face turned grave. "What have you done?"

"You know already."

'Her hand went to her mouth, studying him. She stared, and he prayed she wouldn't make him say the words, wouldn't force him to say he was leaving. It only took her a moment, for as much as he teased, Mary could always work out his next step before he even knew what he was doing. When it dawned, he saw her stomach heave, saw her curl in.

"I knew it the moment I heard it on the radio."

"Mary, I have to."

"They'll blank you when you return, you know that? That's if you come back, Jesus! People round here won't understand why you ran off to help our enemy. Your enemy! No one more than you must hate the British army. We have neutrality, we don't have to do anything, you don't have to leave us, you can stay here, be safe, why stand with them when it isn't our fight?"

"Have you forgotten what you heard on that broadcast? As I recall, you were sobbing all night over what Churchill said. Entire districts are being exterminated, Mary! Thousands of executions in cold blood, he said. I'm not going off to fight with the British, I'm fighting against the Nazis and I couldn't give a damn what nationality stands next to me."

"I was sobbing all night because I knew it changed you. Once you heard that, I knew you would forget about all of us who love you and want to fight for people who have no clue who you are, who will never know you, who will never care. You will fight alongside sons or grandsons of the men who tore your family apart, who made sure your mother never had the chance to love your father, who made it so you could never meet him. Your mother would turn in her grave."

'The man hung his head and nodded.

"She would. You're not wrong there. I'm not doing this for her."

"Who are you doing it for so? Not me, nor the kids, for you'll be leaving us alone. You hardly believe you're doing it for your father, then?"

'A defeated breath surged out of her when she saw his face. "How can you think he would want you to do this?"

'He straightened. Mary could always see right through him, but that didn't mean he couldn't make her understand.

"My father was brave. From what I've been told, he believed in doing what was right. He would've wanted me to stand up to any dictator. Take the English out of it and my mother would have too. They're killing women and children, Mary. Little babies. Imagine it was here. Wouldn't you want everyone, anyone, from any country, to come and fight? You wouldn't care if they were your enemy, so long as they helped."

'She bowed her head, and he knew then she understood. Still, it pained him when she looked back with eyes fit to burst, for he had caused her anguish.

"Surely you're too old?"

"Cut off is forty-one, so I'll make it. I'm fit, and being a recruit for the Irish army already, I'm trained. They'll take me all right."

"You can still change your mind."

'It was as if she read his innermost wish. Yet he didn't show it.

"Not now. I've already enlisted. They've given me a start date. If I do not turn up, they will class it as defecting."

"We could run. I'd live in a ditch if it meant we could stay together."

'He squeezed her closer. "My father would never have run. I have to go. I have to help these people. Can you not see the Nazi's are trying to do what the English did to us? Mary, I can't be a coward as they try to eradicate an entire race. If we were to run, we would have nothing, we would lose our income, our friend's, our family. Here, the town you have known all your life will look after you. I cannot wrench you away from that."

"But I will still have you."

'His face moved southward; the muscles drooped at the enormity of what he had done. At the pain he caused her.

'She laid a hand flat on her chest. She spoke in gasps.

"You've broken my heart. In all the worries in my life and by God there have been many, I never thought you would hurt me, I never believed you would want to leave me, leave us."

'She cupped her hands to his face.

"Until I heard Churchill on the radio and I knew then what my husband would have to do. You have always been the fiercest follower of what is right. It was what made me fall for you, so how can I fight you on this now?"

'When she found his hand, he knew she forgave him. He scooped her nearer, and they sat like that, as close to each other as if they were one person. Until their children grew bored with the fields and came looking for more treats.

'He didn't say all the things he should say. How really, he was terrified. How since he signed up, a sense of foreboding that he might be doing the wrong thing had bombarded his thoughts. How, he had secretly hoped Mary would force him to change his mind. If she threatened an ultimatum, he would have backed down. He should have known better, for his wife would support any idea he put forth as she always had. With an increasing dread, he stroked his daughter's cheek and whooped his small son up in the air and tried to ignore the sorrow burrowing into his heart, the feeling that his life was moving away from him, to unwanted and undreamt of yet nightmares. And then, as the children ran to the river after hearing movement in the grass nearby, Mary cut through his doubts.

'When he was stuck in the trench, with blood pouring from his stomach, the last image he recalled was of Mary cupping his face, while the tears streamed down her own saying, "Edward, you are my life."'

Vicky blinked a few times to stop the brimming tears, then leaned forward. She couldn't stay quiet any longer.

'His name was Edward? Was that your father?'

'No, it was not my father.'

'Why has he your name, then?'

'Because it was me, Victoria.'

Chapter 18

Vicky stood, then paced, then shook her hands out, as if trying to flap the words away.

'You nearly had me there. Why are you telling me ridiculous tales that make no sense?'

'The truth doesn't always make sense.'

'How could you know what happened to a family in the 1900s, *and* in what, 1941, or whenever?'

'Because your great grandparents told me.'

'How? Deirdre got pregnant in 1902, you said yourself her son ... you ... were thirty eight in 1941, that would make you what ... one hundred and twenty-two years old?'

He gave no answer.

'Ah, stop now, Edward.'

'This is what I mean about trust. You only trust what's on the surface, what is in front of you or what you can see, but sometimes you need to suspend disbelief, sometimes you have to put aside the doubt about what appears unreal and just trust the outcome. When we first met, I said you would need to listen, need to trust and I am going to keep saying it as it is your greatest lesson, the one you need the most. You haven't heard the end of the story, of my story. There's more.'

'There's trust and there's being a fool. You asked me to listen and I haven't interrupted, and I'll let you finish, which is a lot more than I'd normally do, so give me a break if I don't automatically nod away.' She splayed her hands out wide. 'Continue with your story.'

Edward didn't acknowledge the sarcasm.

'When I started this, I told you that inside the first story there were three stories. My mother Deirdre's, then the story of how my parents met and my father died, then, now, my life. There are still two stories left. Are you still willing to listen?'

From their first meeting, he had repeated about trusting him, about listening. All her life she had jumped to presumptions, and she was good at seeing the steps ahead, so much so she made a career of it. Every gut instinct, nerve ending, intuition was telling her now to get up, drive him away, drop him off at the hospital and never look back. To close her ears and eyes and forget this whole conversation. To ignore the promise of another two stories.

'Victoria, someone is in danger.'

That was all she needed. She sat back in the chair.

Chapter 19

'On another day, in another person's life, on the second day of November this year, the same trickling sound brings a substitute for comfort, but not enough. The person sits rigid on the mound beside a stone slab, unaware of the beauty of the place, or at least this time ignoring it. They are not looking for comfort, not looking at anything of the surroundings, but searching inside, or hoping for a sign, whether from above or from nature or another visitor. The silence offers them nothing; no indication from above. So, what they take from that is clarity, that the reason they came is right after all, that there is no more need to fight or try or push against what they are feeling. After clarity comes certainty. With each minute they stay, the certainty grows in strength and hardens until it is as weighty as a rock. The belief cemented that what they are doing is right, with no other options. The person looks in that river and their life flashes back at them and they are not happy with what they see. A pitiful life, full of hours, days, months, years and years wasted, and the conclusion they come to is that none of the pain is worth hanging on for. They don't matter. They never mattered. Nobody will miss them.

'The person stands.

'If the tree could talk, if it could project all the good the person had done, it would. The person doesn't see what the river wanted to show them. If only they kept searching, held on a little while longer, life would show what they could do still if only they would live, if only they would carry on.

'The tree knows what is coming but can do nothing to stop the unravelling of events except to groan loudly with the weight; its only way to protest, as its branch leans, as the weary person loops and knots, then finally tugs on the rope. The wind tries in vain to take the pressure from the person's body as they swing, but nature knows too well that gravity always wins. The river, flowing as always, understands it is too late. As the person kicks and thrashes and then grows still and joins the silence, joins the other realm, the tree hangs its leaves in shame.

'The place with the tree sees many things. It is old, spanning hundreds and hundreds of years. The tree sees many people visit and lay under its shelter. If you cut into it, you would see many circles, more than you would ever live. And when we are all gone, the tree will live on. It has been the tree's destiny to outlive animals, flowers, seasons, and humans. The tree has seen the ways of man, been present around love, witnessed men kill enemies, but none of that means anything to the tree.

'All the tree knows is that it likes when someone sits underneath its branches, when it feels a body against its trunk, a life force and energy mingling with its own. It wishes to shield them from the sun, to let its leaves shelter, let its trunk provide support, let the noises of its swaying branches calm. Sometimes it's years before it feels any attention again, but still it waits, and when someone comes, it sees, it hears, it loves.'

Edward shifted in his seat. Vicky tried to make sense of his words.

'How do you know what this is when you don't even say if it is a man or a woman?'

'I don't know who the person is. All I can tell you is what I see and what I see is just what I've said.'

'What does the person look like?'

'It's not clear. I don't see if it is a him or a her. It's like I have a glimpse inside their mind, of their thoughts and then I see what the tree sees, the person's legs, the feet dangling.'

'You told me the date was the second of November. That's in the future, a couple of days away. Are you telling me this because you want me to save the person?'

'Yes. That's why I'm here.'

'Do you know where the tree is?' She stood, ready to leave.

He motioned with his hand to sit. 'Not yet.'

'Why?'

'Because they won't be there until then. Because we are in the middle of a storm.'

'Would you stop talking in riddles, man! Just speak clearly, stop going around in circles.'

'There are things I cannot say. Some facts you have to discover yourself, I am only here to help, to sway you as much as I can. There are many behind me, with their hands on my shoulders, trying to put their hands on your shoulders too.'

'Are you trying to say you knew me before this?'

'I am.'

'But I've never met you. I would remember, I never forget a face.'

'You're right, you've never met me. Today is the first time you've seen me.'

'What is your real surname?'

He sighed. 'Fitzgerald.'

'My father only had a sister, so you can't be an uncle. Are you a second cousin or something?'

'Victoria, I am your grandfather.'

Chapter 20

Vicky shook her head. None of what Edward was saying made sense.

'You can't be. My grandparents all died young, before I was born.'

He nodded, looking at her with that look she had come to know, as if waiting for the penny to drop.

'My dad told me his father abandoned him, not left for war. It's ridiculous to have me believe you could be him. How can you be that age, Edward? It would be impossible to still—'

'Victoria, you are not listening! You are not trusting what I'm telling you. I am your grandfather.'

'Help me understand then! I'm trying to make sense of it, aren't I? What happened after you got discharged?'

'Nothing happened after, not for me anyway, because I never came back.'

He was staring at her again now, his eyes willing her to get what he wasn't saying. 'I never had the chance.'

Vicky tried to make sense of his sentences.

'You died.' Her voice trembled with the truth.

He nodded.

'You are dead.'

'Yes.'

'That's why you keep going on about Samhain. You crossed over. Like the Aos Sí.'

His tone was soft, apologetic even. 'No, the Aos Sí is different. I'm not descended from fairies or gods. I'm family, your family.'

'Is it just for one night?'

He nodded. 'To tell my story, to let you know your ancestors' story.'

'Why though? Why now?'

'Because you need our help. Because your future is our history, too.'

Chapter 21

There was more Edward wanted to say and Vicky didn't have the strength to argue with him so she let him carry on.

'You come from a line of people that fought. It is important you know this, that the reason you have that need in you for justice is hereditary. It is in your blood, in your history. Your ancestors also stood up for what was right. Your relatives also acted brave when they felt fear, for some to their detriment. You have already shown us how you do the same. For my father and myself, that bravery was our downfall. That bravery stripped us of a good life, a long life, took us away from our love. We don't want you to suffer a same fate.'

'I won't.'

He tilted his head again.

Her jaw raised to match him. 'If I don't love anyone, I can't leave them.'

'It doesn't have to be that way though, does it?'

'That's where you're wrong. Haven't I told you already I don't believe in ghosts?'

'This is not a ghost story. It is not some spooky fable about Halloween. What it is, is a tale about the stories that mingle between the living and the dead. How on the night of Samhain there is an opportunity, one chance to gather and connect and, if you listen carefully, you may finally hear the truth about your ancestors. You may finally understand who you really are. We have a lot to teach you, a lot we wish we knew when we were where you are, when we were alive. Take the opportunity to listen, Victoria. I'm not a ghost, I have been gifted a visit, that's all. It is hard to take in, I understand this, that's why you need to trust me.

'I don't *need* to trust anyone. Not trusting anyone has kept me sane. What I need right this minute is some air.'

It only took about two strides to cross from the living room to the back door. As she opened it, the wind whipped the door from her hands and swung it wide. Belting her with pellets of rain, Vicky welcomed the wild weather, for it acted better than a slap, better than she could have given herself to shock her brain into thinking. She ran a lap of the garden, ignoring the wet grass, her slippers sodden in seconds. She needed to breathe fresh air; she needed to wheeze away what had just happened. Had she finally gone mad? Was that what that conversation was? Was Edward even real?

Sure, at the moment there was pressure from work, from closing the station, but stress was always present and she would handle it like everything else, shaking it away as if it was nothing. Yes, losing the station in Knockfarraig would affect her. It wasn't what she wanted but, putting it in perspective, she had dealt with much worse. Or at least learnt to adapt through much, much worse. Was that the problem? Maybe she hadn't handled it at all, maybe she had finally broken? Had the lifelong stress she constantly pushed away formed hairline cracks that joined, splitting the pathways to her brain, breaking reality, stopping cohesion, so she was now sitting in her living room hallucinating, talking to no one but hearing and seeing and acting as if a real person was in front of her? The rain sure felt real. The wind against her face felt real. Edward *seemed* real. In her job, she had witnessed many instances of psychosomatic outbreaks where a person who led a normal life for decades, had just cracked one day and totally out of character done unexplainable acts. Was this happening now? Vicky ran until the veins in her neck pulsed enough to burst, forcing her to stop mid run to catch her breath, afraid if she carried on, she'd keel over. She didn't want to go back in, yet she had to find out if he was really there. The only way to gain an answer was to brave it.

She rewound back over the events of the night; over the evidence she had gathered. The drivers had seen Edward. When he blocked their path, their lights flashed on his body as they waited for him to move. Darren definitely had an interaction; he had told her Edward was getting irate when he tried to approach. The caller that rang Phyllis had, too. The crowd looked straight at him. So, the old man, the ghost, Edward, had been real to more than just her. At that stage anyway. Had a split in her memory happened after, where she dispersed him to safety and was now making up a different version? Or had she cracked before tonight? Was this man just an apparition, a repeat in memory, a flashback of someone seen before, like the way you could dream of a movie star and in the dream the person would be as real to you as if you knew them all your life? With her heart ready to beat out of her chest, Vicky stepped into the house, for she was still the same person, and fear would never stop her doing anything needed doing. Grabbing her baton from the counter in the kitchen, Vicky tiptoed back into her living room.

Sure enough, there was a man there, the same man sitting on the same couch she left him on ten minutes ago, wearing the same clothes she had chosen. She rocked her head back and forth, in case something had dislodged or blocked, and she could force something to the surface.

Edward was still there.

Out in the kitchen, she poured a glass of water and the cold liquid travelled down and hit her stomach. Drenched through again, she welcomed the damp fabric against her skin, hoping it would tether her to reality, remind her of what was real.

'I don't believe in ghosts, Edward,' she said again, leaning on the door frame. It was a sentence that needed repeating.

'Nor I, but here we are. Do you want to dry off first?'

'Give me a second.'

When she returned wearing dry clothes, he waved his hand at the opposite seat, inviting her to sit. Her blood boiled at that; it was her house.

'Come now Victoria, tell yourself the truth. You knew it from the moment you saw me, you knew I knew you. You knew I was there for you.'

She recalled the way he had looked at her on the street. He had unnerved her with his supposed recognition and he was here now, saying he was blood, that he *was* here for her. Her first inclination was to run, but where? For a person who didn't believe anyone, it shocked her how she already believed him. Or was it just that she wanted to?

'If you insist on going over details, I wouldn't class myself as a ghost. Ghosts are haunted souls, apparitions. I am not that.'

He held out a hand.

'You can touch me; you have touched me. Wasn't I flesh and bone?'

He pulled his sleeve up to his elbow.

'Look at the blue in my arms.'

His finger traced the long vein. 'There is blood pumping through this body and my word, never did I ever think I'd have the chance to step into this world again. You said you know all about Samhain, well if you truly know, then you know what it is, for Samhain is an opportunity for the dead to visit the living, to cross over and to tell stories, to say what they never got a chance to say.'

She sat back in her chair, settling herself in.

'What did you never get to say?'

He adjusted his sleeve back over his arm, pursing his lips.

'Too many words. The great tragedy of life is we always believe we have more time than we do. What did I never get to say? All of it. I wish I'd said more, done more, loved more. I wish everyone I cared about knew everything that was in my heart, that they knew all the love I held inside. That I hadn't kept my favourite traits of theirs secret. Take my wife, for instance. Often, when she was unaware, I watched her. Deep in concentration, she would trace her eyebrow with her middle finger. Lost to the thought, away somewhere else. Such a graceful gesture. Until I died, for then I understood she only made that gesture when she worried, about money, or the children, or me. Maybe if I'd brought it to attention, she would have shared her worries more. Maybe she wouldn't have carried the burden alone while I lived. But even that doesn't matter in the end, for we all meet eventually. I've told her now, that's what matters. I wish I'd known worrying is the worst thief.'

'How?'

'Because worrying destroys faith. It robs you of joy.'

'Like, faith in God?'

Edward tilted his head.

'Not necessarily. Just faith in something. Optimism. Faith in life, that eventually everything you want or need will come. Faith that there is something steering all this. That whatever is meant for you will not pass you by. Worrying doesn't help; it only makes a problem worse. If worry is the focus, faith cannot coexist, and if there is no faith, there is no hope, and without hope, you cannot trust. And you, Victoria, need to trust again.'

'How are you so sure I don't trust anyone?'

That tilt again. 'Name one person you trust.'

'Phyllis,' she said without hesitation. Smiling that she had proved him wrong.

His puckered lips moved from side to side as if swishing water in his mouth. 'Not so.'

'It is so. I'd trust her with my life.'

Edward sighed. 'If so, why do you go to the station every evening after she is gone, even if it's your day off, to check she has locked up?'

'That's different. I can trust a person and know she is forgetful.'

'That's not trust. Has she ever left the station unlocked?'

Vicky bit down hard on her lip before answering. 'No.'

'See? No trust. You cannot even see how much it affects you. Or how it changes how you live your life.'

'So what? Trust issues are good in my line of work.'

'You'd think so. At one stage, it did. When you worked in the city, it helped solve cases but did it help you? Not so much.'

He inclined his head. 'Don't get me wrong, I understand why you needed to do this.'

'Come on now, Edward. You expect me to believe you not only have come over from the other side but that you're also a relation, and then what? You know every fact about me and my life?'

'I know your father was hard enough to live with.'

She straightened with the mention of her father, as she did in any conversation his name came up.

'I know he didn't show much love, much affection.'

Edward raked his fingers through his hair. 'This is what I mean about saying the things I should have said. It is my fault he is the way he is. I should have explained to him that day in the woods that just because I was leaving, it didn't mean I didn't love him, I should have explained my reasons for wanting to fight, helped him understand his behaviour didn't cause my decision. He was too young to talk of war, I thought, I reasoned if I explained it would have upset him unnecessarily when it wouldn't have sunk in. Better still, I should have left a letter. I should have considered what it would feel like for my family if I didn't return, but I was superstitious and didn't want to give fate any ideas. Instead, I said nothing, left him with just a pat on the head as I walked out the door. Because of my silence, he grew up angry. Grew up hating himself for not telling me about a dream he had before I left. He started seeing it as a premonition, and it was. Your father had seen me with blood seeping from my stomach, dying in a field. He came to me that morning, crying. Instead of listening to what he had to say, I shushed him, told him he would have to be the man of the house while I was away and to stop the tears because he needed to be strong for his mother and his sister. Only five years old and I made him carry that responsibility.

'It's no excuse, but it was a different time then. Men were told to put on a brave face, stand tall, but I should have gone with my heart that day, I should have held on to my son like every instinct shouted at me. I should have told him how much I loved him; how proud I was to have him as my son. His anger as an adult was all down to me, down to my death. I planted the seed that he shouldn't talk about what hurt him, about his fears. I taught him the people he loved let him down. They went away and never came back. He was afraid to love, Victoria, terrified to give in to the love he felt, or show it, because all the people he loved died when he was young. His mother, my beautiful Mary, died three years later, and then they took his sister from him, adopted her out to a lovely family up the country who only wanted one child. All the people he ever showed love to, left him alone. You know they put him in Artane?'

'The industrial school? In Dublin?'

'That's the one.'

'No, I didn't know.'

'This is what I mean by wishing we say more. If only you knew what he had gone through, it would have all made sense. If only he had explained the reasons the hurt festered, it might have dispelled some, opened him up to healing. He had an awful time, Victoria. You are older now; you know of the things they did there?'

She nodded. There weren't many people in Ireland over the age of forty unaware of what happened in Artane. Known as a place of neglect. Of physical abuse. Sexual abuse. People regarded Artane as a place of horrors.

Edward sniffled, wiped at his nose.

'All you're imagining was done, and more so. My boy, the pain he went through, no one should. He was small for his age, skinny, not even eight years old, all alone in that place. Evil people feast on the vulnerable, they savage the ones that feel alone. He never was alone. His mother and I were with him every step of the way, but he thought he was alone and what you think, what you believe, is what you get. And as he grew up, with each year that passed, with each hurt, he hardened, grew angry at the Christian Brothers, at the Church, dreamt of killing the ones who hurt him, despised the ones who didn't do the damage but looked the other way, hated the other students, the ones that were spared, the ones that picked on him too, him being the end of the pack, the runt of the litter, and his heart grew colder, despising even his sister, the same girl who had cradled him in her arms until they prised them away from each other, because she had been the lucky one, for being the one adopted. He never saw her again. Most of all, he hated his parents, hated me, for leaving him all alone, for not caring enough about him to live.'

'Why didn't you appear to him? Why didn't you crossover at Samhain years ago like you did for me? You would have saved us both a lot of misery if you had.'

'Don't you think we tried? Your grandmother and I tried many a time, but you have to be invited into the person's house to tell your story. That is why I was so insistent; I needed you to let me into your home. Your father didn't trust anyone. There was never anyone he let in. We weren't sure if your distrust had gone too far too, but well, here I am. You proved me right.'

'Right about what?'

He shrugged, looking at her sadly. 'That for you, it isn't too late.'

Behind the wrinkled skin, his eyes were familiar. Indeed, they bore a resemblance to her own father's, to her own even. They *were* Fitzgerald's eyes.

'He's in a home, Edward. Eighty-eight years old with dementia. Is that what you need from me? To bring you there so you can heal him, or make amends? If it is, I'm not sure he will grasp it.'

'He'll be with us soon enough, Victoria, the best parts of him already are, the parts that comprehend. We have made peace with each other.'

'From the other side?'

He nodded.

'It is you I'm here for. To warn you, to help you. The next few days will be tough, the toughest yet. I need you to hold on. To remember what I have said to you when it gets rough. You need to remember to trust me no matter how much it suspends belief.'

'Tough I can deal with, I have before.'

'I know you have.' His words held all the tones of genuine sadness.

'How long can you stay?'

'Until sunset.'

'Tomorrow evening. What happens then?'

'This is all as new to me as you. There'll be signs though I'm sure, messages for me to follow. From time to time a voice guides me. If it is anything like earlier, one minute I was just there. I expect it will be the same when it's time to leave, one minute I will just disappear.'

'Am I just delusional?'

Edward chuckled. 'Not this time.'

She noticed his untouched tea then, the top puckered with milky skin. After, she ran through the beats of the night, searching for remnants of memory from when she offered him food and drink. How had she missed the heaviness as she'd thrown the still full cup away from the garage? How had she overlooked the shakes of his head every time she offered him food? For someone known for her observation skills, she didn't pick up on it. Edward hadn't eaten or drank all night and she hadn't even noticed.

'Can you not eat?'

'If I died with my stomach intact, I could. A stomach injury caused my death so food cannot pass through. The upside is I feel no hunger or thirst. This old creaky body is only on loan.'

'So, you are in a body? Is it your own or are you just an illusion?'

'This body is not my own, for I died at forty. I'm not an illusion, well I don't think I am, anyway.'

She ran through what she remembered of the night, how she had laid the clothes beside him without brushing against his hands, same with the food and drink, never handing them directly to him.

'I touched your head when you sat in the car.'

'You did, didn't you?'

'At least I think I did.'

'There's only one way to find out. It feels real to me, but who I am to say? Do you want to try to give your grandfather a hug?'

'Would you want to?'

It surprised her how childlike the question came out; it was a voice she didn't recognise.

He smiled, his eyes filming over.

'Victoria Fitzgerald, I've wanted to do that since the moment I laid eyes on you.'

Her legs were shakier when she stood than she would expect, the walk to him tentative and full of fear, even though it was not from fearing him as a ghost, or of what he might do to her, but more that the hug would feel real, more that she was giving in to someone else.

As her arms found his shoulder, her breath caught. At that moment, at least, he was living. Her fingertips touched muscle and bone and as her head rested on his shoulder, she could hear breath and her head moved in time as his ribs and chest moved. And with that realisation, Vicky also understood it was now that her problems started, because in her arms was her grandfather and if she believed that, if she believed he was dead and visiting her to tell her the truth of her ancestors, she also had to believe that in a few hours she would lose him again. And that scared her more than anything.

Chapter 22

When they broke apart, she walked out to the kitchen for a moment to compose her shaking body. Once her heart rate returned to somewhere like normal, she sat back in her seat.

'You must help this person, Victoria. Find out who they are, convince them to live, you need to. This person has to be saved.'

'Can you see what will happen if I don't?'

He pursed his lips, then shook his head. 'Not specific details. It's just a knowing.'

She rubbed her temples. 'Right. Let's get clear about what we do know. We know it happens on the second of November. How?'

'What do you mean?'

'I mean, how do you know the date if it's in the future? Is it just a feeling or are you seeing proof?'

'Seeing it. I see a newspaper article.'

'What is the headline?'

He closed his eyes and then lit up. 'It says: Murderer will rot.'

'And it definitely says the second?'

'Clear as day.'

'Okay. And, the tree, is it without doubt the same place where you ate your picnic, where your father died, where your mother married him?'

'Definitely the same place.'

'How do you know?'

'There is no doubt. I know that place better than any other on earth.'

'Then I can do it. If we know the date and place, even if I'm busy I can just send Phyllis there.'

Edward's head nearly shook off its axis with the violence at which it moved.

'No. No one else can fix this except you.'

'How? How do you know that?'

He placed a hand on his chest. 'I just—'

'Feel it. Right. No help, just me then. What is the weather like?'

He scrunched up his nose.

'Come on, Edward, the more details you give me help. Is it night or day?'

Edward closed his eyes again. 'It's overcast. A dull day, dreary and grey. It's hard to tell the exact time. There's no horizon, no obvious hour. It could be morning or evening.'

'Great, so I'm staking out the place for the whole day then. Better pack a lunch.'

'I have the feeling we have to stop what's happening before that, if we want to get through to the person.'

She massaged her temples one way with her fingers, then the other. It didn't work; it didn't take away the pressure; the headache was there and would stay now.

'What details can you see?'

He tilted his head, confused.

'You said you saw legs. Describe them to me? Male, female, what shoes? Are the legs bare or clothed?'

Edward closed his eyes again.

'Not bare skin, I see about an inch of material. The person is wearing dark trousers, either black or dark-navy. Wearing boots, similar to the heavy boots the Germans marched with.'

'Like steel-capped ones?'

'Yes, exactly. They still make them these days?'

'They'll always be a need for steel-capped boots I'd say. Anything else?'

'A few things flash through, random in order and sense. Different things, some aren't in the woods.'

'See them now, Edward, describe them.'

He closed his eyes, and she waited.

'There is a tattoo. On a hand, around this part.' He pointed to the soft pad of skin between the thumb and forefinger. 'Right there.'

'What does it look like?'

He waved his hand. 'I don't know. All it looks like to me is a squiggle.'

To Vicky, this sounded like a familiar tattoo.

'Then I see a face. And I know who it is.'

Vicky leant forward. 'Who?'

'It's the man you were talking to earlier.'

'Which one? Darren? The man that stood beside you on Main Street?'

'The man you spoke to at the place they brought all the people to.'

'Lenny? The guy with long hair?'

Edward nodded.

'It is him in the woods?'

'They feel separate. What I see first is a tattoo. Can't see the person's face. Then it changes to a different place and this man Lenny is there.'

'How do you know it's different?'

'The light. One's harsher, artificial, the other is outside, in the daytime. The time I see Lenny, I only see his face. He looks sad. After that it flashes to a rope.'

'What colour is the rope?'

'The common type, beige, thick. After seeing the rope, it pans out to the place with the tree.'

'Apart from recognising that woods anywhere, how can you be certain it's the same place? A lot of time has passed since you were there, your recollection might have tainted over the years. What if the image you held on to is false? What if the present day woods of your memory are now an overgrown mess, taken back to weeds?'

'Because once you've been there, you will never forget it. You'll understand when you witness it for yourself. Knowing how you doubt everything, I will give you facts: the reason I'm certain is because I see the headstone, I see a finger tap it. Then all I see are those black boots and the swinging. Then a child walking through and they scream and scream. That's it. That's everything I see.'

Vicky grabbed her notebook from her backpack then clicked a pen, ready to write.

'Tell me if it's in this order. You see a newspaper saying murderer will rot, then the date, then you see the trousers and the boots, then the tattoo, then Lenny looking sad, then the rope, then the place by the tree, the tapping of the headstone, swinging, child screaming?'

'Newspaper with the date, then the tattoo, then Lenny, then the rope, the place by the tree, tapping the headstone, the trousers, black boots, swinging, child screaming.'

'Got it. Sounds like we have to visit Lenny.'

'You have to, not me.'

'Hey, we're in this together. Anyway, I'll need back up, otherwise he'll think I'm crazy.'

'Probably best if you don't tell him who I am, not at first, at least. You don't have to say anything to him about what I've told you, just dig a little, show him life is worth living.'

'That's the problem. How do I do that?'

He shrugged.

'You don't have to say anything, but you're coming with me. I'm not leaving you out of my sight.'

'My energy's fading, Victoria, carrying around this old body is exhausting.'

'You can sit down somewhere, I just, I want you near, is that okay?'

She straightened. That was the most vulnerable sentence she had spoken in years. It scared her.

Edward beamed back.

'It would be nice to watch my granddaughter work.'

'Officially, it's not work. I'm meant to be off.'

She looked at her phone, saw the undeleted voice message. 'In a couple of days, I may be out of a job.'

His head tilted again in the way she had become accustomed with him when he wanted her to elaborate.

'My superintendent wants to close the station. Cutting costs, you know? He's another one who believes I have trust issues.'

'And how do you feel about closing the station?'

She blew out a sigh. 'It should make me angry. Normally I'd kick off, but I can't this time. It just cuts into me, makes me feel sad. Really sad. I thought they appreciated what I did here. Obviously not.'

'Maybe you have to show them.'

'There's no point. From the sound of it, they've already made the decision. I don't want to stay somewhere I'm not wanted.'

'What will it mean for you if the station closes?'

'Either I'm out of a job or commuting to the city.' She chewed on a nail.

'Is that a problem?'

'I thought I was done with the city. I don't know if I could go back, if I'm honest.'

Edward stood and hobbled over, then patted her on the hand. 'Don't think too much about it now. Remember what I said about worrying? One issue at a time, yes? Every solution to each problem will come at the perfect moment.'

'I've worked as a Garda long enough to know when someone is holding out on what they need to confess. What have you come to tell me?'

He patted her shoulder.

'All you need to discover is yours to learn. Too much all at once won't be as believable. A little at a time works better.'

'You said there is another story?'

'There is, and I promise I will tell it. The stories will help shift your mind to what you need in your life, to what's been missing.'

'You think there's something missing?'

He arched a bushy eyebrow. 'Don't you?'

Her normal response wouldn't work here. If he'd watched how she spent her days, deflecting the question wouldn't either.

'Have you sat with me in the past?'

'Many times. We get snippets, usually if there is a need. Your low moments are the hardest to witness, for all of us, for we want to interrupt, to let you know we are there, but there is nothing we can do but send love your way.'

'I have never felt it, never felt you.'

He tilted his head, smiled. 'Are you sure about that?'

Chapter 23

For some reason, him doubting her about her feeling a presence over the years, annoyed Vicky more than him telling her he was her dead grandfather.

'Edward, I'd know if I felt you or anyone like you around me before and I haven't, not ever.'

'What about any instinct?'

'Nothing. No sign, no feeling, nothing.'

'Think back.'

She gave a pause, even though there was no need. 'Nothing, sorry.'

'What about when the man hid behind the door? Do you remember what stopped you right as you walked past?'

He waited while she thought. She shook her head, not seeing, not recalling. Until she was there again. Until she knew exactly what he meant. A woman called in about hearing screaming coming from her next door neighbours' house. As Vicky entered the open door, she saw a smudge of blood on the staircase and instinctively crept up the stairs. When she got to the top, she stopped, just about to enter the room with the blood on the handle of what looked like a bedroom door. Now, she understood what he was talking about.

'I heard a voice, not from outside, not from anyone inside the house, either. It came from me. Real clear, as if a person, no not a person, as if I, stood next to me. Saying: *he's hiding behind the door in the bathroom.*

'At this stage, the bathroom door was behind me, so I backed up real quiet. Just as I did, a man attacked with a machete.'

'And if you hadn't backed up?'

'He would have sneaked up on me, he would have attacked me from behind.'

'That was us.'

'Us?'

'Us, yes.'

'What? Like a collection of what, spirits?'

'If you like, but I sense the term spirit is too fluffy for you, too unbelievable. Think of us more like a source of energy. On that occasion we got through because in that moment when you were completely present, you tapped into sound and senses. Fully aware, you could receive what we had to say.' He flicked his hand. 'You don't believe me. Even after my turning up here, telling you my story, you think it was luck that saved you that day, and it was if you reason it out, if you look at it logically. But we tapped into that instinct. We *are* your instinct.'

'Right.'

'Here, let me show you.'

He held out his hand and hovered it in the air, waiting for her to take hold.

Looking at his gnarly liver-spotted hand, her breath hitched, not at the sight of it, but at what he might show her.

She took his hand anyway.

As soon as her palm touched his, the surroundings changed, walls melting into other coloured walls, the carpet changing from plush to threadbare on her feet. Within a second, she was back in that house, the place of her nightmares, the place she avoided all thought about if possible. Inhaling the metallic smell of blood. The hairs prickled at the back of her neck. As if sleepwalking, she tried to lift her hand, but it wouldn't work. Trance-like, she moved. This time she couldn't back away, as she walked up the stairs, cringing as each step creaked, this time there was no stopping. As she passed the bathroom, she slipped on a glove to prevent fingerprints from opening the door. No matter how much she tried to physically step back, she couldn't. This time, she was just a witness. For this time there was no voice, no edging back, no matter how much she willed it, no matter how much she tried to tell herself to not go into the room of her nightmares, she couldn't prevent her gloved hand from opening the door.

It was the same shocking sight that met her in every outcome. There was blood everywhere. In this version, she stepped into the bedroom. The woman's fate already decided, already ended. Denise's body lay hacked apart on the bed. Shocked, Vicky raised her hand to her mouth and let out a sob and the man, covered in his wife's blood, snuck up behind her. All she heard was the swoosh, felt the air cut through with the machete. Felt the cold slice of the blade meeting skin. Then hotness, as the blood rushed away from her veins and out of her body. Darkness followed. Then weightlessness.

Edward's hand squeezed hers.

'That was the other ending,' she whispered. 'It seems I owe you a thank you.'

'We step in if we can,' he said, grinning.

Vicky looked down at Edward's hand. Full of age spots and bumpy veins, gnarly and swollen at the knuckles from rheumatoid arthritis.

'If you died young, why did you come back as an old man?'

'We thought an old man would seem less threatening, so you might give me a chance. Also, once my story was told, for the sake of you to believe me, we felt it was better if I looked like what you would expect your grandfather to look like rather than a man younger than you when he died.'

While still holding his hand, a light flashed between them, once it dimmed, Edward's face had transformed. Now middle-aged, the lines in his face softened and smoothed, the grey hair darkened to brown. Another flash brought him back to being in his eighties again.

'You were the image of my father.'

Edward nodded and squeezed her hand. She couldn't help the tears welling. As unbelievable as the story was, this man, Edward, was telling the truth. Until then, Vicky had waited for a reasonable explanation. Until then she had wanted to find an excuse, a reason, but now the opposite was true, she wanted to keep what Edward said close to her heart. She wanted to take in his words and cherish every sentence. Only in the last few minutes did she understand how limited their time was.

This man was her grandfather.

'Why can't you stay in the younger version of you?'

'Because I have to stay in the body I chose. They allowed a flash, but nothing more.'

'Did you die straight away?'

His smile didn't reach his eyes, and she knew he was thinking of a way to soften his answer. 'A few hours and it was over. You bleed out quickly from a stomach wound. It wasn't pleasant, there are better ways to go, the pain at the end was all-consuming. Pain never lasts. No suffering is ever permanent; it all ends eventually.'

'You didn't have to go to this much trouble. I would have listened.'

He smiled again. 'We have tried before.'

'Are you serious?'

'Do you remember when a woman asked if you could hide her in your house?'

Vicky stopped. 'But she was being abused by her husband. I drove her to a refuge in Crookstown, a great one that was better than anything I could do for her.'

'On that occasion, we didn't count on the speed of your efficiency. We tried to put a few spanners in the works, but you fixed it all within an hour. That's why there had to be the storm tonight. It had to be an old, vulnerable man who wouldn't harm anyone but himself.'

'What is so important?'

'Someone will die if we don't step in. There is a pattern occurring that if it happens, you will lose someone very important, someone integral to the path of your life.'

'Can you show me? Can you do that thing with your hands again?'

'We can try.'

He held out his hands. When she took them in her own, they were as cold as a slab of marble. This time there was no flash, no vision. They stayed cold.

'I cannot summon it.'

'So, what do we do?'

'All I can do is tell you about the past, in the hope you may change your future.'

'And there is something in my future I need to change?'

'Something big is coming and you have to be ready.'

Chapter 24

As if the clocks started up again and the night unpaused, the shrill sound of her ringtone broke through their conversation, making them both jump away from each other, and release their hold.

She looked around for her phone, spotting its illuminated screen on the side table.

'I have to check that. The station diverts to my mobile,' she said.

'Course,' he said.

The number wasn't familiar or in her contacts. 'Garda Fitzgerald,' she said.

'It's Lenny here, from the Youth Centre.'

'Your number isn't the same.'

'I'm ringing you from the office.'

A loud noise erupted in the background, like a roar.

'We have a problem with a person staying here. I've tried calming him down, but he's getting more aggressive and I don't want to kick him out into that storm. If you're far or off duty I understand, I can ring the city, it's just, seeing someone in uniform might do the trick and one lad thought you might know the fella.'

Vicky bit down on her lip, looking at Edward. He nodded, giving her permission to say yes.

'Bet you it's Harry fighting. Trouble follows that man around no matter how much he protests otherwise. Give me five minutes.'

She hung up. 'Looks like we'll be seeing Lenny sooner than we thought.'

'Not we, you.' Edward held up his finger at her crestfallen face. 'Occupying a body again is exhausting, same with talking, I could do with a rest. Don't worry, we have time.'

'Not much.'

He smiled. 'It will still be enough.'

'I wish I could stay.'

He squeezed her shoulder. 'It is happening exactly as it should. There is never anything accidental or by coincidence. This is all part of the plan. Some of your learning needs to be without me. Anyway, you need the idea of all this, of what I have told you to settle. A reprieve from my stories will do you good. You have heard all you're ready for. The rest will come before I go, don't worry.'

'You sure?'

He nodded.

'Fine, I'll get dressed for what must be the tenth time tonight. Anything I can get you?'

'Do you know what I'd really love?'

'What?'

'I'd love to listen to the old songs while I'm here. All you lot listen to these days are the computer stuff, never the old style. Do you know what I miss the most about living? Using the senses. The chance to touch, the sounds, the smell of everything.'

She grinned. 'That I can help you with.'

She turned on her smart TV and chose a long playlist of music from the thirties.

Edward chuckled as the notes played, clicking those thick knuckled hands along to the beat. 'Now that's what I'm talking about.'

After she changed into her uniform, she lit some scented candles and dotted them around her living room, then picked up an extra cushion and tucked it behind Edward's back. He slid his back from side to side.

'Heaven.'

'You'll be safe here on your own?'

'As safe as a dead man can be,' he said, laughing.

As she closed the door, her foot dangled in mid-air instead of stepping down. A blast of wind took the breath from her. With shaky hands and a thumping heart, she shoved the key back in the lock, then burst into the room again, heaving breathlessly even though she hadn't exerted her body. Edward was tapping the arm of the couch, his fingers moving to the beat, his eyes closed in bliss.

'You won't disappear, will you? Promise me, Edward. Promise me you'll be here when I get back?'

He opened his eyes and smiled. 'Trust me.'

Chapter 25

The first noise coming from the Youth Centre didn't sound like a gun going off. It was more like a pop or a drop of an object on the floor. The second brought alarm, making it undeniable. Someone was firing. Three teenagers at the entrance instinctively went to run, putting her hand to her mouth to warn them to stay quiet. She mouthed, 'Sit in the car.'

One teen nodded so fast his head was in danger of vaulting from his neck.

'Go then,' she said, handing over the keys, and with her permission they ran, not caring about the wind, rain or storm. She didn't move until they locked the car.

As she opened the door to the Centre, the sounds of shouting whooshed towards her. Standing in the little room covered with leaflets, there was only one direction the noise was emanating from. No other voice shouted back. It was the loud sound of dictatorship, of someone who had grown in power, who had gained an audience. A threatening voice, almost a bark, giving the impression the dispeller was unstable. Underneath his outbursts were undertones of other sounds now: the catch and sobs of a woman, of different women, the shuffle of feet on the ground, the scraping of belts from lying awkwardly in various areas of the room. The skin prickled on Vicky's neck when she realised this wasn't just a man spouting off. Something more sinister was at play. As she was just about to burst in through the double doors, she stopped.

Edward's earlier conversation replayed. About the man that hid behind the door with the machete, about how the voice inside had guided her. Taking a large intake of breath, she allowed her breathing to shallow, calming her fit-to-burst heart, softening the surge of adrenaline.

Think, Vicky, think.

Going against what she would normally do which was run towards, she stilled, she waited, silently speaking to whoever might be listening.

Tell me what I need to know.

Although the words were not spoken out loud, she heard them as if they were. Spoken in her voice, to her. And then the same voice answered.

Those doors swing inwards.

What did that mean? She edged closer. Tipping one door slightly with her finger, she made a slight gap. People crouched on the floor or lay or sat against walls. One woman nearest the door lay face down with her legs twisted at uncomfortable angles, as if she rushed to get into position and couldn't move. A man, tall and stockily built, paced past. He had one arm upright and when he passed again a few seconds later she saw the glint of metal.

Shit. What is it about you and doors?

Vicky directed the question to the ceiling, even though she knew the person hearing her wasn't up there but sitting in her living room, reading her mind. This time there was no answer.

The man stopped right in front of the doors. His wild hair sprang out in all directions and nearly blocked his hand holding the gun. He aimed it straight up in the air. As soon as she saw his hand rise, Vicky didn't need any prompt, or any other sign from Edward or the Divine or a source of energy, for what happened next was calculated and pure instinct, pure her. With her full force, she shoved the left side of the door, making it jut forward and knock the man off balance so he fell flat on the floor, scooting across the wood. Running after him, she took hold of the gun before he hit the ground, where he lay for a few seconds in shock. Not realising the gun was gone, he tried to fire it, straight at her, making the motions into the air with his fingers. The crowd, realising he could no longer harm them, let out a collective sigh and some, standing to their feet, found their voice again, found their courage again and got ready to attack. Vicky pointed a finger at the worst of them, warning to stay back. Doing so, she took her attention away from the person she should have been watching, so she missed it when he got to his feet, then shoved her. She fell down hard on her hand, splayed out to catch her fall. The gun scooted away. As she reached for it, the full force of the man landed on her back, pushing her head to the ground. Fingers clawed at her hair, yanking her head back with the severity. Her focus stayed on the gun, her fingertips stretching to touch the cold metal. The man noticed too and scrambled over her body to reach it first. Then his weight lightened, and she was free again. Lenny lifted the man in the air in a headlock. Depositing him in the furthest corner of the room, like he was a pile of clothes. Harry rushed to help Lenny settle the man. The same Harry she had assumed was the troublemaker.

Harry and another man held him down. Within seconds, Lenny picked up the gun and disarmed the bullets. On any other day, this would have impressed Vicky, but it took every bit of effort to not pass out.

'You got cuffs?' Lenny asked.

As she tried to remove the cuffs from the pouch on her belt, she moaned. Lenny knelt on the floor and released them.

Two lumps protruded out from her palm. No sign of a broken wrist, as far as she could see, but the bruises were already forming, attempting to heal. It hurt just as much as if it snapped.

Lenny cuffed the guy like it wasn't the first time, then lying him face down on the floor, he rushed back.

The pain was too much to lean on to stand up. Lenny extended his hand. The gesture, the look in his eyes, she couldn't decipher. Was it concern or sadness? A ripple in her stomach. Was it another sign? Was it a warning? Those dark eyes wanted to instigate multiple conversations with no words at all. They asked if she was in pain, if she needed help; they asked her to trust him. There was something more too, something she didn't want to know, something she said goodbye to years ago. She looked away. But, she took his hand with her uninjured one. He pulled her to standing. Immediately, she stepped back, not wanting to be up close.

'What happened?'

'He turned up after you left, asking for a bed, so I got him settled. Everyone was getting ready to sleep for the night when he riled up, saying someone stole his bag. A few of us started searching and the next thing you know, he's putting a hole through the roof of the Centre. He lost it.'

Only when the man turned his head did she see who he was. The hair was wilder than it had ever been.

'Archie. He's a regular at the station. There's a history of mental illness, but he's never acted violent before.'

With that, high-pitched screams started from the face-down Archie.

'Could you sit him up so I can have a word?'

After Lenny uprighted a screaming, kicking Archie, she sat facing him, keeping enough distance.

'Don't worry, you're safe.'

Too agitated to focus, his eyes were glossy, flicking from side to side, above her head and face, away somewhere else.

'They robbed me, took my things, all my things, important items I need. They have no right, it's my stuff, my important stuff. No person should touch my bag, my personal property, I don't go around touching their things. I want my bag back; I want my property.'

'And we'll work on getting it returned to you if you promise to behave from now on. What did the bag look like?'

'Orange with yellow birds, you can't miss it, it's unique. No one else will have one like it.'

'That sounds about right.'

He jerked his upper body, trying to yank himself up onto his feet. 'They took it! I have to get it back. They have no right. It's mine. No one has the right to touch my property.'

She steadied his shoulders.

'Archie. Breathe for me.'

He jittered and rocked; his head jerked from side to side, looking around. Vicky leaned forward.

'Don't look anywhere else or at anyone else. Remember me? How's your cat doing, the guy who likes the salmon?'

This caught Archie's attention. His eyes flickered to each side once more, then aligned, meeting hers. 'Willow. Willow loves salmon.'

'Gorgeous cat, Willow. You're good with her, kind, and she's mad about you. A cat gives such love, don't they?'

He nodded. A sound of a cup clinking distracted him, made him jerk his head to look around again. Vicky needed to grab his attention. To keep his attention.

'Remember the last time we met you were worried about Willow, when you had to go to hospital, you worried she would starve?'

This did it. A shift, a change of refocus took place, as if he was only seeing her for the first time that day.

'Do you remember what I promised you then, Archie?'

In the background, Vicky heard Lenny dispersing the crowd, aware he was settling them, soothing as much as she was trying to soothe Archie. They made a good team.

He shook his head warily, not recalling.

'Remember how I promised I would go to your house and put some food and drink down for Willow? Do you remember I did? That I kept my promise, Archie?'

He nodded, played with the thick stubble on his chin. 'Do you remember how I proved you can trust me?'

He shrugged, getting bored now.

'So, I'm going to need you to trust me again. We are going to look for your bag, but you are going to have to stay still and not cause any more trouble. Will you do that?'

Archie twisted his body, lifting his cuffed hand nearer to her face.

'Look what Willow did. She was only playing, like, she never means to hurt me but she gave some scratch.'

Vicky traced her fingers along the red welt by the metal cuff.

He sniffed. 'Archie didn't mean to shove her out of the way. Archie never hurts Willow; he never hurts his friends.'

'Willow knows that. Will you help me now? Will you stay still?'

He nodded, rubbing his head against one shoulder.

'Did you eat today?'

He shook his head.

'Stay there and I'll grab something for you. Be good, promise?'

'Promise,' he said, going back to stroking his head against his shoulder.

As if sensing her presence, Lenny turned as she neared. 'You took some jolt. How's your hand?'

'Been better. Any food left?'

'In the kitchen. What should we do with him?'

'First, we'll give him some grub. Best bet with Archie is to keep him distracted. If he's left too long with his thoughts, he can implode. Next thing I'll do is ring the nearest station. With this hand I can't drive him, the distance is too far, so I'll need them to come out. He can't stay here, he'll only fire up again.'

'What about Knockfarraig station?'

'Isn't an option. It's closed for good in two days and anyway I've a feeling it's underwater.'

'Why? Closed for good, I mean.'

She held her good hand up.

'Pick one. Government cuts, not enough crime, and a consensus that there is no need for my services. I could go on but won't bore you. While I'm figuring out where to put Archie, if you could search for the bag? It should stand out, he said it's orange and yellow. With birds.'

Lenny raised an eyebrow.

'We'll see.'

She pointed at the door. 'Kitchen, yeah?'

'Go on ahead. On the bottom shelf you'll find loads of offcuts of meat. You'll find bread in the top cupboard. I'll watch Billy the Kid.'

'Thanks,' she said.

'Should be me saying thanks. When I rang, I didn't know he had a gun. It turned pretty hairy before I could react. You're our saviour.'

Vicky couldn't help herself. She took a long look at the whole of Lenny.

'You look like you can handle yourself.'

In the kitchen, she felt like she took a breath for the first time in an hour. What was it with this night? Checking her watch, it shocked her to read it wasn't yet eleven. Lenny's voice travelled from the other room, and she smiled at the way he was calming but giving out roles at the same time. There was comfort in the way he said things, for it was a voice with authority that didn't cross the line and evoke fear. It was reassuring; *he* was reassuring. With only one workable hand, making the sandwich proved harder than expected. Never one to give up though, after considerable time, she laid the plate on the floor in front of Archie.

'Am I right in remembering you love mustard?'

Archie grinned, showing gum. She removed the cuffs, then took his hands and cuffed him to the front.

'Good, I slathered it on. Eat up now and we'll find your bag. I've cut it into small pieces so you can pick it up.'

She sighed as he tried to pick up a piece of sandwich with the cuffs on and her heart went out to him. The system failed people like Archie. It shouldn't be a cell he was going to tonight. He shouldn't have needed a bed at all, especially not on a night like this, in the storm. Society, hospitals, family and the government had turned their back on this man.

'What were you thinking, Archie? Where did you get a gun from?'

'Found it,' he said through a mouthful of bread. 'I didn't think it was real until it went off. When it did, I kind of got distracted, got kind of power hungry like.'

'Found it where?'

'You know farmer Mike? He brought me to his house for dinner and he said make myself at home. There was a big cupboard with a load of all different types on the shelves. Big long ones and short bulky ones. The metal looked all shiny, I just wanted to hold it in my hand but then he came back and I didn't want to say I opened the cupboard so I hid it in my jacket. Then I liked how it felt in my pocket, it made me feel safe. And strong.'

'Don't you think taking the gun is the same as someone taking your bag?'

'No way! I was planning on giving it back the next time I went for dinner. Which is the first Sunday of the month. Ask farmer Mike, I never steal, not ever. I was just hiding it and then got carried away.'

Vicky made a note in her notepad to check if farmer Mike had a gun permit.

'I'll look for that bag.'

Back in the kitchen, she flicked on the kettle and made the phone call to the station, out of earshot from Archie, then opened cabinets to check for the bag.

As she was just stirring the teapot, Lenny stood at the doorway. 'One bright orange bag with luminous yellow budgies is now sitting with its proud owner.'

'In fairness, Archie never lies. Did someone nick it?'

'No. Or if they did, they thought better of keeping it after his outburst and hid it in the jacks. Archie's checked inside and seems happy that whatever he wanted was there.'

'I'd better get out and make sure there's no more weapons.'

'No need,' he said, stopping her. It was just a hand on her shoulder, yet it felt like a jolt. Like something to take notice of.

'I already did a sweep before I gave it to him. All that's in there is a bunch of newspapers, some well-used, dubious-looking tissues and a radio. Want me to pour that for you?'

'Actually, I was making us both one.'

'Allow me,' he said, scooting past. 'Let your hand rest awhile. What did the station say?'

'I only got through to the Garda at reception. Seems like they are having as crazy a night as us. They're going to call me back.'

'How's your hand?'

'Sore, but I'll live.'

'Can I look?'

She nodded, but didn't meet his eyes. He cupped her hand and lifted it as if it would shatter at the softest of touches. Lenny's fingers slid over every knuckle and bone. She braced, expecting pain. His strokes were careful enough to only tickle. Vicky closed her eyes. Even though she knew what he was doing was functional, that he was only checking for lumps or breaks, it didn't feel that way. Even though his fingers barely touched her skin and were clearly on a fact-finding mission, she couldn't ignore the tickly bristle of the calloused pads of his fingers and the gentleness of his touch. Satisfied with his discovery on the topside, he turned her hand palm up. Between his thumb and forefinger, in the loose skin between, was a shape – a slanted line starting from where the thumb ended with an arch that reached back to the edge of the soft flesh. Her stomach lurched. A tattoo on the spot Edward described. A shape that Edward might think was a squiggle.

'That needs ice,' he said.

'I'll be fine.'

'Stop a moment, let me help you.'

She met his eyes then and, as they stood there facing each other, with him cupping her hand, she forgot the pain and remembered desire. Remembered wanting desire. What would it feel like if he reached down and kissed her? He seemed so together. Sturdy. Irresistible. At that moment, Lenny seemed the least likely guy to wrap a rope around the branch of a tree.

Still holding her hand, he opened the drawer beside him and took out a packet of painkillers. Picking up a glass by the sink, he turned on the tap and filled it with water.

'That's impressive. What you can do with one hand. Maybe I could have tried it myself?'

'Shush,' he said. 'I've a strong feeling you never let anyone help you.'

He popped a tablet out of the sleeve and, holding the packet up to show her the brand, gestured to her mouth.

'I can take it in this hand.'

His eyes widened in warning, then gestured with the pill again.

She rolled her eyes but obeyed, dropping her mouth open. Lenny laid a tablet on to her tongue, then rested the glass on her lips.

'Ready?' he asked, his eyes on hers.

She shook her head no, but he dribbled the water into hers, anyway.

The phone rang. She swallowed the pill back. 'See, I told you they would ring,' she said, relieved to have a distraction. Lenny leaned against the fridge.

'Garda Fitzgerald?' The person on the line asked. She watched Lenny bend down to get to the freezer and turned her back, not needing any more distractions.

'That's me. Is that Ballinroe?'

'It is, I'm Garda John Houlihan. Sorry about the delay. You need assistance?'

'Under control as such, it's just I've hurt my hand so can't drive to the station with my ... cargo.'

'Is he a danger?'

'Not now. He's cuffed and compliant but might not stay that way for long. Really, he's better in the hospital, but according to weather watch, the road from Knockfarraig to the hospital is impassable. He just needs somewhere safe to sleep where he won't come to harm or do any, either.'

'A cell we have. Between you and me though, we're swamped. Tons of people had to abandon their cars and need help. Judging by the line here, the earliest one of us will leave is two hours.'

'Two hours?' Edward's time was ticking by. 'I can't wait that long.'

Lenny picked her hand up to hold the ice pack in place and mouthed, 'I can drive.'

On automatic, she shook her head no. Then she thought of Edward and her need to get back. Where would a refusal get her? She would have to stay in the Youth Centre for hours. Also, she knew how worked up Archie could get. It was best to get him moving, get him away from the crowd of people. It was best for her to get home as soon as possible.

'Look, if I get him to you, can we speed up the paperwork? I'm going to have to get my hand checked out. I'll dictate my statement on a voice note or something.'

'Don't worry about the paperwork side of it. We'll sort it later. How will you get him there?'

Vicky looked at the hand on hers. 'I'll manage.'

Chapter 26

Archie stepped into the Garda car with no resistance. After stuffing himself with two more sandwiches and a generous wedge of cake, he was in no mood to pick a fight. His only movement being the occasional rub to his bloated belly. With him safely deposited in the back, Vicky was about to sit in the passenger seat.

'Hold on. You'll need my jacket.'

'For what?'

'If anyone sees you driving dressed like that, they'll think you've taken me hostage or something. At least if you're wearing the jacket, they'll assume you're one as well.'

'Understandable, although I don't think we'll meet many cars out in this,' Lenny said, taking the jacket from her. 'Anyway, I don't think it will fit, you're way slighter than me.'

'That one is extra big. Even if you can't tie it, it has to be better than nothing.'

She giggled as he struggled to get his arms inside.

'Extra big, my arse,' he said, laughing himself.

'Will that crowd manage without you?'

'I made a call to Alayne, she works in a place on the Main Street. She knows the guys. She'll look after them.'

'Alayne Adams?'

'That's the one. You know her?'

'Everyone in Knockfarraig knows Alayne. Especially anyone that needs help.'

His lips drew a line. About to say something, she busied herself with her seatbelt.

'Could I get arrested for impersonating an officer with this?'

'Come on now, this is Knockfarraig, not New York you're talking about. If you drove to the station in a tractor, they wouldn't care.'

'That's all I want to hear. Once I have a verbal statement from an officer, I'm covered.'

'I'd give you a written one, but don't think anyone would understand the writing.'

'You're a lefty?' he asked, nodding at her hand.

'I am.'

'I've never met a left-handed person before,' he grinned. 'You're special, aren't you?'

She checked behind her to make sure Archie was behaving himself, hiding her smile. 'Just drive, will you?'

The model prisoner, Archie's eyes were already closed, with a slight snore coming from his exhale. Safe to talk, she settled into the seat, needing to distract from the pain in her hand and also, if Lenny was the person by the tree needing her help, there was no better way than to get him to tell her about his life.

'So, what's your story?'

Lenny kept his eyes on the road but tilted his ear closer.

'In what way?'

'What way is there? Start with how you ended up working in a Youth Centre?'

Lenny pursed his lips, then took a deep breath. 'Well, when you take all the wrong turns, you eventually learn how to take the right ones.'

Vicky stole a look at Archie.

'Not the case for some people. Many never find the right ones.'

His eyes widened. 'Too true. If I can stop the boys making half the mistakes I made, I call it a win.'

'Is that so?'

He shrugged.

'That's the intention, although it's hard to let go of the ones I can't get through to. At the start I thought I could just show them or tell them my story and they'd get it but I've learnt that isn't always the case, a person doesn't learn necessarily by anyone telling them what they should do, they have to come to their own conclusions, have to figure it out themselves. Sometimes you can show them the lesson so they experience the moment. The more I work in the Centre, I see it's not always easy to just show them or talk to them. I keep learning, keep plugging away, hoping one day it will get through.'

'Are you one of those mythical creatures you hear about sometimes?'

He shook his head, confused, keeping his focus on the road which was vital with the amount of debris flying around.

'A good guy.'

'Depends on what you mean by good, I guess. If you mean someone who screws up often but spends his life trying not to, then yes. Any level above that then I'm sorry to disappoint. If you're looking for a guy who's never done wrong, that's not me.'

'I'm not looking for a guy at all.'

There was a long pause.

'I didn't mean you're looking. I just meant I'm not perfect.'

'Got it.'

He brightened. 'Long way from perfect. Just ask my two sisters, they'll give you a long list of my faults.'

She tapped the side of her head. 'Mental note, ask sisters just that.'

The rain lashed against the windscreen. Lenny leaned forward. Him having to concentrate on the road allowed her time to study his face without being caught. There was stubble on his jaw, black with a few flecks of grey in part. Exactly the type of man she would pick up in a bar if there were no consequences after. Exactly the type of guy she would run away from the next morning. He had a lived-in face. Fine lines etched by his eyes. Laughter lines, she hoped, although she knew from her own that trauma could cause them just as easily. He caught her looking and looked right back.

That was the difference. Most people didn't look at a Garda straight, they avoided the eyes like she had a clairvoyant power or something that could glimpse straight into their soul. Even the most innocent of people avoided her eyes. Not Lenny. He looked right at her.

'You trying to save the world, Lenny?'

'Look,' he tapped the steering wheel. 'When you've done as many bad things to people as I've done, hurt as many as I have and then you want to make amends, it takes a lot to try to make a dent.'

Vicky made a mental note to do a quick background check on this guy.

'Anyway, you should know more than anyone what that's like.'

'How so?'

'Surely that was a reason to join the Gardaí? To fight crime, keep the streets safe.'

'Nah. I just joined for the annual promotion and pension plan.'

Lenny snorted at the joke.

A flash of lightning followed a crackle of thunder. She jolted. There was nothing Vicky hated more. Snowstorms, hailstones, even the dead heat of summer in full Garda uniform never bothered her, nothing fazed Vicky except the threat of a lightning bolt. It was pitch dark now, right into the deepest part of the night. She wished she could just return to her living room and speak to Edward. The tick of the clock was at the back of everything. She needed to get home.

What should have taken five minutes in the station was like everything else in these places: long, drawn out and unbelievably boring. The whole time she waited, conflicted thoughts filled her mind, jutting from wanting to be both in her car and at home.

Eventually a tall, flustered-looking Garda came to the counter. 'Vicky?'

'John?'

'That's me. Sorry to hold you up. How's the hand doing?'

She held it up for him to see. Swollen and bruised, it was unrecognisable from her other hand. 'Been better.'

'Ouch. We've got a first aid kit here if you want to make use of it?'

'Nah, taken the painkillers and just want to get out of here, no offence.'

'Ha, I'd go too if I could.'

The station was way fancier than Knockfarraig. Money was thrown at this one. Bright lighting and warmth wafted as soon as you walked in, though Vicky would take the cold and the dinginess of Knockfarraig any day over that. This type of station she had no wish for. Two drunks slumped in the corner, both swaying to their own internal beat. Three women with big hair and even bigger voices were pointing fingers at the officer behind the partition, demanding to have some relation released, as far as Vicky could make out. Twenty more sat on the floor looking like there was nowhere else for them to go or anywhere else they could be.

Once all the usual booking-in procedures were out of the way and the gun was safely handed over, John ushered them into a room at the back and Archie, in fairness, didn't show any aggression, except for a flicker of his eyelashes when John took the bag, a flicker Vicky knew well. She placed her good hand on his arm.

'They'll make sure they give it back. John promised me he'll lock it behind the counter and watch it all night. It's safe here.'

'What about Willow?'

'I promised, didn't I? I'll stop by your place.'

'If I'm here ages, she'll starve.'

'Don't worry I'll check in on her every night until you're home. Okay?'

Archie nodded and went to his self-soothing gesture of rubbing his stubble.

Once checked in, after she sent the voice note and signed what needed to be signed, John had it processed in ten minutes.

'I'll leave you go get that hand checked out.'

'Thanks,' she hesitated, instead of moving.

'You need something else?'

'I was wondering if you could do a background check for me.'

'Sure. What's the name?'

'Lenny.'

Vicky stopped. Edward's word repeated to her. *Trust.* Also, she realised she didn't know his surname.

'Never mind.'

'You sure?'

'Yeah. It'll wait.'

She could have added that this time she would try to be different, that this time she would trust someone, when every other time she didn't. Or that really, she had no viable reason to check out Lenny except for her deep mistrust of the world. Vicky didn't explain how life had given her reason to, that it was hard to believe anyone out there could be who they said they were, that she had discovered in this job how even the most respectable of people have secrets, and how those were the most shocking.

For once, Vicky wanted to find out about Lenny the old-fashioned way. The right way. She would give him a chance to tell his own story, as much as she was dying to know what made him tick or how big his big mistakes had been. In that alone there was something, a dropping of resistance. She smiled at the thought.

She whispered, *'Can you see me now, Edward?'* and then, *'I'll speak to you soon.'*

Chapter 27

Outside, the rain had relented and only the wind remained as a reminder of the storm. Despite the wind, Lenny sat on the bonnet as if he was chilling on a summer's day. He spotted her as soon as she hit the street, his eyes lighting up. He was just a man sitting on a car bonnet, but the surprise of him doing that, that he was waiting for *her*, made her take a step back. There weren't many things or people that she could say scared her, but this guy put her on edge, made her shackles rise. Was it instinct? Or was it fear of letting another in? His smile was contagious. A chuckle escaped her as she reached him.

'You know doing that's an offence?'

He tugged at the collar of the jacket.

'Not when I'm in this uniform. You've given me free rein to do loads of things I've always wanted to get away with. What would happen if I turned on the siren going home?'

'I'd have to arrest you.'

'Cuff me then, officer,' he said, turning his arms and offering his hands.

There were marks on the inside of his wrists. A long line running down the middle of the arm, following the vein. Welts saw too often in her line of work. Slashing across was often a cry for help, following the vein was usually a final act. Seeing her notice, Lenny dropped the grin and his hands.

'If I cuffed you, I'd have no lift home,' she said, softer than she usually spoke to him.

'We'd better go,' he said.

In the car he busied himself, embarrassed. Vicky placed a hand, the good one, on his arm. Instead of jerking away he took a deep breath, then twisted his body slightly, leaning closer. Not enough to be considered a come on but enough for her to know if she leaned in too, something might happen between them. Instead, she edged back.

It wasn't part of the rules, her rules. And anyway, if Lenny was the person who ended up by the tree, she needed to delve in further, get to know him more, become a friend even. Being attracted to him wouldn't help the situation. It certainly wouldn't save Lenny, knowing her track record with relationships. Before, she could see no reason for him to end up as the person in Edward's premonition, but after seeing his wrists she understood, in his past at least, Lenny had a history of searching for a way out. She would need to tread carefully, not dive into a one-night stand.

'Thanks for helping. I couldn't have got through this night without you.'

It changed the atmosphere, made him sit back, pull on his seatbelt, buckle in. Once done, he smiled, a casual gesture of genuine affection, but it was like a whack – Lenny's eyes lifted when his mouth turned upwards. Vicky felt a stirring.

'Least I could do after you saving the day. Only reason you're hurt and in this situation is because of my call. I should have handled it myself. When he started kicking off, someone mentioned he was harmless and that you knew him, so I thought he might calm down on seeing you. If I'd known he had a gun ...'

'You did the right thing. Honestly. Archie panics if he's backed into a corner. He's erratic on a good day, let alone with a weapon. He could have easily killed someone waving it around and the sad thing is he wouldn't have meant to, he's just one of those lost to the system, one of those that didn't have a safe place growing up as a kid, no direction, no attention, no love. Maybe something like your youth club is the answer? Maybe you can change the direction of their life early on.'

'That's the hope.'

'Anyway, you were right about the familiar thing. He doesn't respond well to strangers.'

'Easy to be right when you recognise the feeling.'

'That's what I can't work out about you; you don't seem shy.'

'Not shy ... just not confident, not happy in my skin, in my abilities, in who I am.'

'Am?'

He smiled. 'Was. It took years to look folks in the eye.'

'Yeah?'

'Yeah,' he said, taking his eyes off the road and focusing on her to prove his point.

'No problem now. Or is this just a show?'

'Don't have the energy for shows or pretence. I am who I am these days, sometimes I'm fine with that, other days, not so much. My greatest battle in life has always been against myself.'

'Go on. I need more.'

'Like, do you ever have days where you just wonder why the hell you've done something? Acted that way, talked like that, chose it. Sometimes I just annoy myself so I can't imagine why anyone else would stick me. No matter how many good deeds or how much I try to help, I just, never really liked myself, I guess. One on ones are never a problem, I'm good with them, especially if I've got to know the person. This night might have given you a false impression of who I am. Believe it or not, I'm actually quiet around people.'

'Not with me.'

He laughed. 'True, I keep asking myself why is that?'

She shrugged, then winced when she banged her hand off the car door.

'Maybe we're kindred spirits. On a night like this, staying quiet moves to second place. What with the storm and having a man waving a gun at us, it would be hard to stay strangers.'

He shifted his shoulder closer, glancing her way. 'That's the thing, though, you don't feel like a stranger at all. Even from our first meeting, it wasn't like I recognised you, I'd never seen you before yet it felt like I did, like seeing you standing there brought no surprise, as if it was perfectly natural for us to talk to each other.'

Just to avoid him, she wiped at a smudge on the window.

'Without trying to sound cheesy, I feel drawn to you.'

Vicky laughed. 'That sounds cheesy as fuck.'

Lenny scratched at his beard. 'It does, doesn't it? Hearing the words come out of me, I nearly upchucked. I promise I've never used that line before in my whole life. All I mean is, I don't know why, but it's like something is pushing me to stay around you, like I have this urge to tell you more, to want to tell you more and for me, that's rare.'

Vicky didn't answer, couldn't answer. Didn't want to ruin his sentence with a stupid "me too". Because me too wouldn't be the right answer when she didn't understand how she felt at all. How in just one night the appearance of two men in the space of mere hours had made her question the way she'd lived her life for thirty-six years. Confirming she felt the same would ruin how she felt, would filter it, and for a little while she wanted to sit with the new feeling. For once, she didn't want to look at someone else with the same eyes she had viewed the world for so long. This time, she wanted to see a man softly. Without harsh judgement or harder vision. She didn't want to search out the catch or dig out the dirt. With him, without questioning it too deep, she wanted to know more too, but she wanted to do things differently. She dared to look over.

The eyes change when attraction, or love, is involved. They soften, caused by the person softening, when skin crinkles and lips curl. It is a glimpse at truth, at another person's truth, when two souls lock eyes and what they separately want meets in the distance between, when the world around with all its chaos fades, turns into a symphony playing in the background of their story. When you know you are there, that you exist, for that precise moment, a moment you have waited for. When you feel nothing else but the importance of it. Right then, all you see is the person's eyes and they are looking at you, seeing you, deep inside your stare. And then it is gone. Either when a thought rushes in, or a sound reminds you where you are, and you realise that you can't keep staring at this stranger.

Vicky didn't say what she was thinking: that she wanted to know all of his story, wanted to know what made him smile or cry or want to get out of bed in the morning. It was stupid, but an urge to ask him what his favourite breakfast was came over her. Instead, she bit down on those thoughts. Love ruined everything. She shifted slightly towards the window, away from him.

'Will you be all right to look after the Centre tonight? I need to get home straight away.'

'What about your hand?'

'Nothing a nightcap and some more painkillers won't dull. It'll wait until tomorrow.'

'I can drop you to the hospital now. It's no problem, I'll—'

'No. I need to get home.'

'Someone waiting for you?'

'Yes,' she said and knew what she was doing when she gave no explanation. As handsome as Lenny was, as much as she felt some push towards him, even if tasked by Edward to possibly save this man's life, or convince him life was worth hanging around for, sleeping with Lenny wouldn't change the outcome.

Vicky didn't want him.

Chapter 28

Outside her house, Lenny turned off the ignition, then handed her the keys. The street was a mess; as if a giant pulled a tree from its roots and used it as a saltshaker, leaving bits and pieces of leaves and branches. Rubbish too. Before they parked, Vicky had to get out of the car at the start of the street to pick up a bin that was being blown around as if it was only a piece of paper.

'Thanks for the opportunity to break the law and not get arrested.'

She laughed, more out of relief at breaking the tension than at his joke.

'Don't make a habit out of it. Next time I catch you driving a Garda car I'm arresting you.'

His smile turned. He bit down on his lip, as if stopping himself from saying the thing he wanted to say. Just like she had done.

'You all right, Lenny?'

'This night has been something, hasn't it?'

'You could say that. Thanks again.'

'My pleasure.'

She raised an eyebrow.

'Not that I get pleasure from you being in pain or people being stranded from their homes in a storm or anything like that, it's just ... I don't sleep well, so anything that distracts me from staring at the walls is welcome.' He shrugged at her questioning stare.

'Nightmares?'

'Sometimes. Flashbacks more. When they come, I'd rather be awake then deal with them. Other times, when I lay down, all the things I did wrong come to the surface and I can't let them settle, I have to get up and do something. And here I go again telling you insecurities I've never said before.'

She ignored the last sentence.

'Some kind of trauma?'

'Ha.' His laugh punched the air. 'You could say that.'

The force of the wind shook the car strong enough to nearly lift the wheels. They both swayed too.

'You can't walk back to the Centre in that and I can't let you drive the car without me. Why don't you come in for a while? I'll ice my hand again and after the swelling goes down, I'll drive you back or we could order you a taxi if they are running again. Unless you need to get back to the Centre straight away?'

He shook his head, looked right at her. 'Alayne texted to say it's all under control, lights are out and most people are snoring.' He tapped the glass, didn't look her way. 'Warming up for a while would be good.'

They both got out and ran to the door. It didn't surprise her to see no sign of life from outside. Presuming Edward could witness their conversation she had the feeling he wouldn't wait up. Sure enough, he'd turned off the music, the lights too, with no sign of him at all in the living room.

'Hold on a second,' she said to Lenny and went checking the other rooms. She found Edward lying on the spare bed, with his eyes closed. Satisfied he hadn't disappeared; she clicked the door shut softly.

On the walk back to Lenny, when she pictured the way he had just looked at her in the car, she felt a stirring inside. Edward wanted her to save this man, but how?

She startled. Lenny hadn't sat down. Lenny was leaning against the wall, between the living room and the hall where she had left him. For a person always on alert, where he stood wasn't what startled her, rather the way he leant against it, with his hands behind his back. It was the eyes, though, the way those eyes followed her, the way they searched as if digging around for answers she didn't hold. There was something else inside that look too, as if he was desperate to touch her. As if he was waiting for her to move. She didn't speak. He didn't either. She kept walking until she was against him. Body on body. Lips on lips. Stubble grazed her chin, and oh, how she had missed the burn. He grabbed her behind and lifted her up. That was new. At her height, no man had tried to lift her before. She wrapped her legs around him, only breaking away from his kiss to point him in the right direction to her bedroom.

There, they ripped at clothes, undressing quickly, but still too slow. Lenny was careful to remove her sleeve over her hand.

'Do you want this?' he asked.

She pulled at his lip with her teeth.

'I want this.'

She led him to her bed. Fumbled in her locker for a condom. Then, throwing it at him, lay in the bed.

'Humour me, but do you mind if we turn out the lights?'

She didn't add that she was worried if someone might be watching.

Give us some privacy Edward, she thought.

For a brief few minutes, she forgot all that came before. All that she usually held on to. All that she carried around. For a few blissful minutes, Lenny replaced the pain. Replaced *him*. Before the guilt flooded in, before she pushed down her feelings, before she hated herself again, she felt peace.

Afterwards, they fell asleep like as if switching off a light, with Lenny still inside her, both of them still joined. He didn't move away or push her body off, just held her still wrapped around because the pull of sleep called to him too, something neither of them usually were capable of, but together, neither needed to watch out for the dark.

Chapter 29

A branch kept scraping against her window. Another indistinctive sound pulled her from her bed, made her open her door and go outside her house, padding barefoot onto her road. A woman with long white hair, dressed in material that billowed and flapped in the wind, appeared by her side. Her face etched with wrinkles; folds of skin burrowed into bones. A cloak covered most of the woman's face, bringing shadows and darkness into the concaves of her features. Focused only on the ground, oblivious of Vicky's presence entirely. At first, the woman moaned softly, then her voice hummed, growled even, catching in the throat. Vicky could hear the rip of the vocal cords as the volume rose and turned from a growl to a shriek, a sound that could pierce both hearts and eardrums. Then the woman clapped, a slow beat to her steps. There was a prolonged rhythm, slightly off beat enough that it kept you on edge, expecting the last to be the last until it wasn't, startling her again. The shriek was one long word. *Victoria.*

She ran to the house and closed the door, only looking back once to see the old woman settle by a large oak tree, kneeling down by the roots, with her hair splayed on either side. Vicky closed the door, her whole body shaking. She sat on her chair, afraid if she didn't, her legs would go from under her. She squeezed the spot between her eyebrows. There was a bang at the window that nearly sent Vicky up out of the chair to hit the ceiling. The hairs stood on the back of her neck. A tapping followed the bang, like a branch against glass. Then scraping, tinkling.

'Vicky, for Christ's sake, would you ever get a grip?' she said, shaking her head.

Another moan. This time muffled, travelling through glass. The clapping was there again. Vicky placed her hands over her ears, willing it to stop. The sound repeated through her window, clearly a woman's moan now, soft and full of pain, repeating over and over: Victoria, Victoria, Victoria.

She woke in a sweat, a clammy film over her skin. Shaking, Lenny was holding her, watching as if he knew what she had just dreamt. The night was still black. The wind still howled.

'You were crying out.'

She broke free of his hands, for old habits buried deep. Lenny flinched. Raking her hands through her hair, she avoided his stare.

Vicky winced. She forgot about her hand.

'Let me see,' Lenny asked, scooping it from under the blanket. 'It's quite swollen. We should go get it checked. If we take the back roads, if we …'

'Stop, Lenny,' she said, removing her hand from his grip. 'There's no need for trips to the hospital. I don't have time.'

'It looks pretty nasty though; do you want me to get you some painkillers?' He flipped over his side of the duvet and swivelled his legs out of the bed, unaware or undisturbed by his nakedness.

A heat rose up her neck at the familiarity of his gesture.

'No, it's my house, if I want painkillers, I'll go get them myself.'

Lenny shifted his body. 'Sorry, didn't mean to overstep.'

'I'll survive. Once it's not life threatening, it doesn't bother me. On the scale of past injuries, it doesn't even hit the top ten list.'

Lenny nodded. 'Now I'm not sure whether to get back in the bed or get dressed.'

Vicky hit her back off the headboard, trying to find the words. Still shaky from the nightmare, the intimacy from only a few hours before had disintegrated. 'Look … I'm sorry.'

'That means get dressed then.' He covered his groin with the sheet as if suddenly noticing his nakedness.

'It's just, Knockfarraig is a small town. We'll have to run into each other.'

'We hadn't before.'

She roughly smoothed out the duvet.

He swivelled, then brushed her cheek. 'Who hurt you, Vic?'

She flinched, flicking his hand away with her cheekbone. 'Show me an adult who hasn't been hurt. Doesn't mean anything.'

'Not anything. Everything. If you hold on to it.'

She leaned away to look at him. 'You only know me five minutes and you already see how messed up I am? I thought I was better at hiding it than that.'

This time Lenny trailed his finger the full length of her cheekbone. Vicky suppressed a shiver.

'When someone's been broken, they can recognise it in others. We carry the pain.'

She tapped her chest. 'You think I'm in pain?'

'Not think. Know.'

'No, you *think* you know. You know nothing about me, Lenny. We are strangers and this conversation is ensuring it stays that way.'

'Look, I don't want to push you away. I just, I wanted you to know I get it. I see it. See you.'

'People see what they want to see. Believe me, I come across it every day. You could ask ten witnesses what a suspect looked like, who'd only just ran past, and they would all give you a different answer.'

'That includes you, you know? Seeing what you want to see.'

'How is that now?'

'You want to see me as disposable, right? Someone you should regret.

You want to downplay what happened between us. Downplay your feelings, but I don't think you can, really. I think if you were honest, what happened between us was as different for you as it was for me.'

'Different isn't necessarily good.'

'It felt good. Didn't it feel good?'

She bit her lip. 'Something can feel good and be a once off. Some things you shouldn't repeat.'

'Like?'

'I don't know. Bungee jumping, passing an exam, getting married. It's like ice cream. I could happily eat that for breakfast, lunch and dinner, but I'd die of a heart attack before I'm fifty.'

'Good analogy comparing me to something that will kill you. Anyway, who said anything about putting pressure on each other? It's not like I plan on slipping a noose around your neck.'

She startled at his choice of words. Lenny carried on, oblivious.

'No need for labels, no relationship talk, I can't stand adding pressure either, we could just keep it natural. We both live busy lives and have our days filled, I'm sure. It's just that ... I like being around you. We could go slow. Meet when suits you.'

'You say all the right words, Lenny, but you're missing one important factor.'

He flopped his hands in his lap. 'Don't, Vic. Don't give me the brush off here.'

'I just like to keep my professional life separate from my personal. Usually, I don't like to mix the two. It can get awkward.'

He shifted on the bed. 'Doesn't need to be. If you want what happened between us to be forgotten, I'm a grown man, I can do that. It's only awkward if you let your head get in the way now.'

She tilted her head, actually looked at him. 'Sorry. Habit. It's just we don't know each other.'

'If you ever want to get to know me, you know where I am.'

She thought about Edward, about the tree. 'Maybe give me time?'

Lenny stood and Vicky didn't avert her eyes, allowing herself one last look at his naked profile. Her groin almost groaned at what she was giving up. Her head won. She patted the mattress.

'Hey, sit back, will you?'

'No need.'

'Look, I'm not trying to kick you out, it's just the timing is off. There's someone here with me in the house. Remember the old man in the Youth Centre earlier? Well, it turns out he's my grandfather and he can't stay long, just one more day and that's it, then I won't see him again.'

Lenny stopped dressing.

'Like ever?'

'Like ever. So, I have to soak up as much time with him as I can. This, between us, whatever it is, doesn't come naturally. My instinct is to run but I, it's important you understand this time, with you, I don't want to kick you out.'

She covered her face with her hands. 'Lenny, I'm saying I want to get to know you too.'

He prised her hands away, kissed her soft on her lips.

'Understood. That must have killed you to say. If it's time you need, it's yours. I should get back to the Youth Centre, anyway.'

'Hold on. It's still sounds bad out there, I'll give you a lift.'

He zipped his fly, turned around. 'Nah, the walk will clear my head. The windier the better.'

A sentence brought back a memory. Of a time with someone else. A time when she was happier. *What was she doing?*

'Lenny, I'm sorry, I didn't mean for it to go like this. I always ruin things.'

Lenny sat on the bed, traced the line of her nose. 'You haven't ruined things, haven't ruined this.'

He leaned in for a kiss.

What was she thinking? This was too much.

She pulled back before he made contact. 'No, what I mean is I ruined it by starting it.'

Lenny drew back. His smile couldn't cover the hurt.

'Look, I'm sorry, believe me, I'm doing you a favour. I'm messed up.'

'That makes two of us.'

'Exactly. How can two messed up people end up good for each other? We'll only rip each other apart. I can't do it, I'm sorry.'

He waved his hands as he stood. 'No need for sorry. We had a good time. At least I can say I got to drive a cop car. That's one bucket-list memory I never imagined ticking off. See you, Vic.'

'See you, Lenny.'

And then she let him go, right into the rest of the storm.

Chapter 30

The Rules:

Never sleep with anybody from Knockfarraig.

If you sleep with someone, it can only be for one night.

Never, ever, stay over.

No matter what, no second meetings.

Chapter 31

Acting unsurprised by her entrance, Edward lay awake in the bed like she knew he would.

'Lenny gone?'

She nodded.

'Rough sleep?' he asked, heaving his body to sitting.

Her arms hugged her body from the memory. 'Nightmare.'

'Tell me.'

She shook her head. 'I don't want to waste words on it.'

He tapped the edge of the bed. 'Try.'

She sat. Edward stayed still, waiting for her to speak, his expectant eyes, shiny orbs, trained on her in the dark room. She thought about arguing her point about not wanting to talk about it, then resigned herself to the fact that the old man had way more patience to sit in silence, so she gave up the fight.

'There was an ancient woman with long white hair. She was moaning and—'

'Clapping?'

'Clapping, yeah.'

He shifted his butt, straightening his back to the headboard.

'The banshee. Whose name did she say?'

Vicky shook her head. 'It was just a dream. A nightmare.'

'Whose name?'

'Mine. She said mine.'

Although shaken before, Edward's fear now chilled her to the bone. To break it, she laughed. 'It was only a dream.'

'Do you believe that?'

'Well, you obviously don't.'

'Your life is in danger, Victoria.'

She shrugged. 'Nothing new there. I'll deal with it.'

'Do you think that is what you've been doing? Dealing with it?'

She turned so she could face him while sitting, shifting one leg across the other on the bed.

'What do you mean? I'm here, aren't I? Anyone else would have run a mile when they heard your story. Most people, normal people, wouldn't have listened to you, but I did. I—'

'What you're doing isn't living. It's a slow death.'

Her mouth dropped open, then when she realised it, she closed it again.

'A slow death. Are you serious?'

He waved his hands in the air. 'Where are your friends? Where are the people you love, Victoria?'

'Hold on now, I—'

The waving arms flopped down on the duvet, causing her to stop mid-sentence. The sound of his hands slapping against material acted like smelling salts, waking her up from an unconscious state. Where *were* her friends? There wasn't one person she could swear she loved.

Edward leaned forward, placed a gnarly hand on his chest, the knuckles swollen to twice their size, his fingers curled instead of straightened.

'I know the pain you experienced. The things you saw, the horrors, I can't erase. But you took that life and squandered it and tried to hide behind your job here in Knockfarraig. It isn't enough, as much as you tell yourself it is.'

She wrapped her arms around her waist once more, suddenly cold.

'At least it's safe.'

'You tell yourself that's why, but it isn't, not really. You're the bravest Fitzgerald there ever was.'

That heated her up. It was her turn to wave hands in the air.

'Then what? If you know me so well, why did I leave the city?'

'Because failure scared you more.'

'Failure? Please.'

'Tell your truth, Victoria. The lies people tell cause most hurt.'

She moved from the bed to sit on the chair so she wasn't as close. Edward was annoying. Going on at her for not accepting what he was saying. Tell her truth? What did that mean? She folded her arms to ward his words away.

'As far as I knew, that was my truth, Edward.'

He was having none of it.

'How has Knockfarraig ever kept you safe? Search inside that stubborn head of yours. Fiddle around in there. It might need some dislodging, but it'll come. How has Knockfarraig ever kept you safe? Or should I say your loved ones?'

And then she knew where he was going with the conversation.

'I can't, Edward. I can't talk about him.'

In the dark, Edward leaned forward and laid a hand on her knee. She felt the concern; the care seeping out of this man. She closed her eyes, overpowered at the level of love sweeping over her.

'Isn't it all about him? All the hiding, all the staying away from people, keeping them away. Knowing everyone in the town but making sure they don't actually ever get to know you, except recognise you're the person wearing a uniform. And it's all a disguise so they don't find out that you bleed too, that you cry, that you hurt as much as them.'

'No. That's not true about staying away. Nobody wants to get to know me. They all view me with suspicion, no one wants to be friends with the "pig".'

'Before I tell you the next story, I need you to tell me one. I need you to talk about Christian.'

'That I can't do.'

'You have to. It's time, Victoria, can't you see? You can't keep him locked up inside, hidden from your memories. Have you not wondered if that is the reason I'm here? Memories have energy. They have the power to turn your outlook negative or positive. They can take you back in time.'

'No one is locking him up or hiding him. I think about Christian every day.'

He wiggled his finger, saying without saying it wasn't the truth. 'Only the end. What I want you to remember is the beginning. To remember the good.'

'No.'

'Yes.'

'Edward, you don't understand. I physically can't. There's a block there, an amnesia. I can only remember the end and once that is present, nothing else can be brought to the surface.'

'When I met you, I asked you to trust me. You need to let people in, to learn to trust, even if it means trusting yourself to remember. Remembering the good doesn't mean you will get hurt again. It doesn't mean you're vulnerable.'

'That's exactly what it means. I did it once and look where it got me? You say you were around, well, it destroyed me. I nearly didn't make it.'

'If you don't let in the good, what is your life worth? Nothing beautiful can make its way to you unless you let go. You are blocking what's meant for you. Don't you see? Can't you see?'

'I cannot speak of him.'

'Why?' Edward asked.

'Because if I say his name, if I share a memory, it is no longer just mine. It mixes with other people, joins other stories, or loses its significance with opinions they have of him. It doesn't stay just mine. Or just mine and his. And then it disappears until it's gone.'

'It will never go.'

'It will,' she argued.

'The pain will fade, but the love will stay. Always. Love never leaves you and what you had, Victoria, was real.'

Even though the tears welled, she wouldn't let them spill. 'It *was* real. Still waiting for that pain to fade though, Edward and it's been years.'

'That's because you are keeping it active. Every morning you remind yourself of how you should feel.'

'So what? You're suggesting I forget about him? One minute you are saying it was genuine love and the next you're telling me to swipe what I felt for him aside.'

'You will never forget Christian, that is never an option. When you experience love, even if it ends badly, you carry the memory for the rest of your life. That is why the loss is so heart wrenching; your natural state wants to feel it again. Come on now, Victoria, you're better than that. Tonight can change everything.'

'How? It's not like you can force him to come back. All this, bringing it up. So what if that's what I've done? He left me and it was the only way to cope, to push it all away, to push anyone away meant I could survive it or end it. I didn't end it, I didn't quit, surely that matters?'

'You may as well have died.'

She held her chest, shocked at his harshness.

'I know what is inside you. Don't you get that yet? I feel your feelings, understand every thought. Dying would have been understandable with the love you both had. Hearts stop over less. It wasn't like death scares you, you weren't frightened to end it all, and fear didn't stop you either. For you, death was too quick. Instead, you suffered. You live on so you can hurt, so you can act out a self-set penance, and that isn't right. He doesn't want you to suffer.'

'You're chatting to him now, is it? Call him up there so and tell him

I'll put the kettle on.'

'You jest, but you know what night it is.'

There was no more resistance. No more fighting against. Her hands touched each other, palm to palm, as if in prayer.

'Edward, please. If you can, do.'

Chapter 32

'I'm here to help you heal, Victoria, not summon anyone.'

She shook her head. 'He haunts me. I don't believe in ghosts, I told you that, yet his ghost has lived with me for a very long time, Edward.'

'I know.'

The pitch of her voice rose higher, almost in panic.

'I don't think I can let him go.'

'You don't need to. That's what you don't understand. You can live and he'll still be around. For you, he'll always be around.'

He placed his hand on hers. It was a dead man's hand, cold and waxy, yet she didn't shudder, because she needed the cold to keep her conscious, to keep her from slumping with the shock.

'If you're ready to hear, it's time for the third story. This one will be different, though, for I will not tell this one. For this story, I will show you.'

There was a question inside his statement. Those expectant eyes waited for compliance or refusal. There she sat, afraid of what was to come, the seconds rolling along and turning into minutes. She considered shaking her head, standing up, running from the room, sticking her fingers in her ears and hiding under her duvet until the man disappeared the next day. But where would that get her? What might she hear in this tale? She took a deep breath, steeled herself.

Vicky squeezed his hand in agreement.

Chapter 33

A flash of light, followed by a whooshing. Hard plastic from the steering wheel, with a searing pain in her head. Icy water sliding onto her lap, splashing against her legs.

Her first thought was of him.

Confusion at the passenger seat, at the emptiness where he sat only minutes ago. No sign of him in the back, either. Water coming in fast, too fast, pouring in from a hole in the windscreen. Everything was black. The river water as cold as sitting in an ice bath. Before her body went into shock, she needed to move. The door wouldn't open, wouldn't budge, as if a thousand walls were against it. With one last breath she followed him, followed through the hole in the glass he must have made, her scream made bubbles as she caught her thigh on a shard on the way out. Not knowing that scar would be a constant reminder of the night, the sight of her crepey skin too much of a trigger to look at years after. At the time, it didn't matter, she was happy to let it rip all her skin away, as long as she found him.

Through murky water full of floating pieces made from coins and glass and moss and dirt and her own blood from the gash on her thigh, she searched, until her lungs begged, until she couldn't take it, when the lack of available air closed in, compressed against her chest, wrapped around her throat, she rushed up to the surface. Sucked in delicious air. With great gasps, she scanned the river. There, she spotted the last of the car as it bobbed, a corner of the boot resisting submergence. On the water's surface, broken pieces of wood floated from where the car hit the fence. Water bottles, leaves, her Garda hat, but not him. Across the entire surface of the river, there was no Christian. Her breath jagged, through rising panic rather than grappling for breath. She had to find him. Scanning above, she figured out where they entered the water, analysed the lines on the grass where she slammed on the brakes, in case he catapulted in the sky before they hit the lake. They had both looked at each other when they knew nothing could prevent them from going in, just before they went over the cliff. There was fear in his eyes and she tried to look strong and was about to say 'don't worry,' when they hit the tip of the rocks that jutted out, and the car flipped. Just before she hit her head on the steering wheel and lost consciousness, there was a juttering, then a cracking, a splintering then a splitting, followed by the most terrible whooshing sound she'd ever heard and that was it, the blackness took her until she woke up.

As the car disappeared under, she scoured the rest of the water, checking to see if she missed any spot, in case anything else bobbed on the surface but there was nothing. The panic expanded in her chest until she was sure she would die of fright and the water was so cold she had to fight from passing out as she screamed his name at the top of her voice and for once, when she needed it most, all reason left and she had no clue what she should do. Her limbs were turning to ice and when she tried to go under to look for him her body wouldn't work, it wouldn't move and when she dipped her head under it was like a million red-hot needles pierced her brain and arms and legs and her eyes stopped working, the cold turning them blind so all she could see was black. Lightning flashed in the sky and yet still she couldn't see under. Time was running out. She screamed his name over and over until there was no sound or energy left and the numbness overtook, pulling her down into the water. By then she knew it had to be too late and there was nothing left to do but join him, to go to wherever he was so she closed her eyes and left fate take her to her love, to her death.

The darkness brightened; the water replaced with the warmth of her house in Knockfarraig. Her chest heaved as she struggled to breathe. Edward was beside her, rubbing her back.

'Breathe, Victoria.'

'I can't ... I don't want to.'

'That's not true.'

'It is! I don't want to live without him. I wanted to die; I should have died that day with him.'

'It surprised you when you woke up in the hospital didn't it? But, also, do you remember the relief? Do you remember the guilt you felt for knowing you survived when he didn't?'

'Yes,' she said through her tears.

'Here is what Christian wanted you to see.'

Edward lay his palm flat, open as an offering, inviting her to take hold. More than anything, she wanted to trust him, but she was terrified of being hurt again, of trusting and regretting it, of being let down, of putting her faith in another person and them failing. Before trusting, she wanted to ask if what he showed would help her, wanted some guarantee that it would heal. Edward smiled, his silent way of asking again. As soon as she took it, she plunged back into the water, the cold knocking her breath away. Her limbs, her throat, everything constricted and then she understood, Edward was giving her this gift, allowing her to die with Christian, allowing her wish and it was all she wanted, to cease breath, to follow her love to wherever he was now and, as her lungs flooded, she felt her life seeping away, her energy and will draining, leaving.

Then floating.

Not floating on the surface, but lifting, becoming lighter, becoming void of any weight. Turning into a spectator, like before in the house with the man with the machete, she separated from the woman, from herself, a different woman from the one still floating in the spot she had just been. Now she was bone dry, only a witness. From the grassy bank, she observed the moment the woman, her, went completely under, saw the moment she gave up, gave in and accepted her fate. Lightning struck, illuminating her surroundings. A head, then a body, flashed on the far side on the right. Vicky ran over to the mound on the ground and there he was, face down, hidden from the water by some long grass, his eyes still open, the fear in them captured forever, already dead, his head bashed in at the side from the impact, from the windscreen glass he broke with his body, that would become her saviour, would become her exit.

Her knees squelched against soft mud as she lay her body close. She stroked his face, lay her head on his shoulders, on that body she had once kissed every inch, that knew every centimetre of skin. And then she roared with every bit of breath she had in her lungs.

Christian was dead. The love of her life was gone.

And then Edward transported her back to the muddy bank away from Christian, her knees clean and mudless again. Edward appeared beside her. He waited until her chest stopped heaving, and she could talk again.

'I couldn't have saved him,' she whispered.

'No, you couldn't. There was no pain in his death. You have the proof of that now. No matter what you would have done, he would have died, Victoria.'

He nodded towards the water. 'Watch.'

The river was a sheaf of black glass. She followed Edward's gaze, towards where she had been, to where "past Vicky" still was. Her body had completely sunk, only tendrils of hair floating and skimming left, until even that plunged down.

This time, a light flashed. Not from the lightning; it wasn't even coming from the direction of the sky. It flashed from the right, came from Christian, then hovered above where his body lay, like a million blue dots, like minuscule particles of light, that evaporated from his corpse and became air. They lifted out of him and up, until a floating mass formed across the sky, stretching out in a line of particles that hovered over the surface, over the area that the woman in the water had disappeared. As the tip of the blue particles touched the surface, the whole river illuminated and became transparent, revealing the shapes underneath, fish and every plant below lit up, displaying their colours. Unconscious Vicky floated down, resting on the riverbed. Above the surface, the particles joined until they took on the form of Christian again, a bright-blue Christian, not of this earth, shimmering, made from only the loosest of atoms. He entered the water, flowing down until he reached the body on the riverbed. The blue moved under her, cushioning her contact with the muddy surface. Loosening again, the particles wrapped around her until they conjoined, became one form. They pushed Vicky up, lifted her until they broke the water. The blue atoms rolled along the surface with her body on top and they moved towards the mud until they deposited her on the riverbank.

Vicky, the witness, went to stand but Edward held her arm and shook his head as he pointed. Staying still, only a foot away, she watched her motionless past self. Even though she knew the outcome, knew that she would live, she hadn't known this, couldn't believe this. The blue atoms fused until they made a vague human shape and, for one exquisite second, the form turned almost human. Christian looked right at her, at conscious dry Vicky. He smiled. When she tried to move to run to him, she found Edward's arm made her immovable, made her frozen to the spot.

Christian bent over; the top of his head touched unconscious Vicky. It looked like he was kissing her, kissing the sodden, lifeless girl. As the blue particles touched her mouth, her lips slightly parted, and the water gushed from them into the middle of Christian, but didn't stay inside, instead the liquid pooled through the atoms, landing on the mud, forming a puddle beside them both. As the last of the water filtered into the puddle, past Vicky spluttered and breathed again, her skin turning red from the exertion and cold. Sirens sounded in the distance. The particles of Christian separated until each one became a separate blue light source, only about a centimetre apart. Then they moved, sliding upwards, as if the law of gravity flipped and they could fall up, as if they were being sucked into the sky. There was another flash, and the atoms joined the lightning and they were in darkness again.

'It was the lightning that night that made the deer startle and run out,' Edward said.

'I should have knocked it down.'

Edward tapped her thigh. The gesture soothed her.

'You never would, even if it happened again or a thousand times over. It's in your instinct to save any life, even if you know the love of yours will die because of it.'

'He *was* the love of my life.'

'It's important you know he was there with you. It's important to know you couldn't have saved him. He was dead as soon as he hit the window, Victoria. The glass splintered his temple and pierced his brain. He would never have survived even if you'd got to him in time.'

'They told me that, but I didn't believe it. I thought he might have swam to get help and the glass pierced him then.' She turned to Edward, felt for him in the dark.

'What if he was driving?'

She clawed at Edward's shirt. 'Could you do that? Could you change it or make us switch places? Because he deserves to live more than me, he was always better, he was the good one.'

'That's not true.'

'You asked earlier about why I left the city. Well, you already know, you said it was about failure and you were right, I failed so many there. How many died because of me?'

'You can't save everyone you meet. You couldn't save people you didn't know.'

'My entire job is about keeping people safe, Edward.'

'So, you fail when anyone in the town dies?'

'Yes!' she shouted. 'You saw for yourself that woman cut up. I should have known that man was dangerous. I should have removed Denise from there.'

'You didn't even know her, Victoria.'

'But that's just it, don't you see? I should have. In a small town like Knockfarraig, I can keep tabs on everyone. I can check on the ones struggling, I can follow up, talk to them when they are low, give them a hand.'

'At who's expense? Isn't it exhausting trying to hold up a whole town? But wasn't that what you wanted when you came back here? A way to sleep, to collapse into bed each night so the nightmares wouldn't come? All this time, you've been asking the wrong questions. You shouldn't have listed the people who died, who you believed you failed, you should have been asking how many lived because of you.'

She shook her head and was about to answer no when the grass and the river disappeared and changed to a large stage, with the riverbank she was sitting on replaced by a cinema seat. Velvety soft, with armrests and space in front to stretch her legs out.

Within seconds, a line of people appeared on the stage. At first, they all looked like strangers, but then some familiar faces popped out. A woman stepped forward.

'Alice,' she whispered.

Edward appeared in the seat to her right.

She furrowed her brow at him. 'What's this?'

He inclined his head. 'You remember her?'

'Alice is a woman I brought to the station and gave some soup to last winter. Don't tell me she died, Edward?'

'What you don't know about Alice is what would have happened if you didn't bring her in that night. Do you remember the ice on the windows that night, how it froze on the glass?'

'Yes.'

'If you died in that river the same night as Christian, Alice would have died that night last year. There would have been no one looking out for her, no offer of soup, no warm sanctuary of the station, no phone call made for emergency housing. Do you understand?'

'I guess, but we don't know that someone else wouldn't—'

'Anyone else you see?'

She scoured the crowd. A woman with blonde curly hair and a scar on her jaw caught her eye.

'Robin.' As she said her name, she smiled. 'I always wondered what happened to her.'

'Because of you, she has her own home now, away from that man, away from the husband that would have murdered her. Do you understand, Victoria? You made a difference to these people's lives.'

'Why is Lenny there?'

Edward screwed up his nose in confusion. 'I can't see the future. Maybe you have already saved him?'

'I don't know that guy,' she said, pointing at a guy wearing a beanie hat.

'You stuck up a poster on the bridge with a list of numbers on it.'

She waved her hand for him to carry on.

'After a suicide there, you designed a poster with your own number, along with the Samaritans and some others. Do you remember what you wrote on the poster?'

She smiled, remembering. 'This is your sign to keep living. Talk to one person first.'

'That man.'

The man in the beanie hat waved.

'He didn't ring you, but he took it for the sign you intended. Skipping the first, he rang the second number on that piece of paper and once he spoke to them, they gave him the exact words he needed to hear. He left that bridge that night alive because of that sign.'

Vicky smiled. 'I went for shock value. Got some ear bending for that one.'

'When something like that works, you never hear about it. This man, Adrian, he's your proof that it did. Do you recognise this girl?'

He pointed to a young girl, shy and unsure. At first, Vicky couldn't place her, not until she flicked her hair. In an instant she could see her, back in the car, sat beside Richie Collins. The girl who wouldn't testify against the man claiming Vicky broke his arm.

'Another girl only alive because you lived. If you hadn't pulled Richie out of his car that night and arrested him, two hours later he would have thrown her body over the cliffs into the water.'

'I knew I was right about him.'

'You changed the course of all their lives. You helped every person here, Victoria.'

Embarrassed, she changed the subject.

'Why do you keep calling me Victoria? Nobody does that?'

'Because that is your name. A good name gives strength to a person. How can anyone with a name meaning victory be anything but strong? Written in your destiny, declared and intended by the people who loved you.'

Vicky scoffed. 'I don't think it was thought about that deeply.'

'How do you know?' Edward shocked her with the boom in his voice. 'How do you know what your parents felt when they came up with that name? You know nothing of what your mother saw when she laid eyes on her daughter for the first time. You took her breath away, not just with your beauty but with a resilience she could see even then. She whispered into your ear, "You know everything already, don't you?" Your eyes were wise and not yet hurt. You looked right back at your mother, and she swore you were telling her she would be all right, with a look full of certainty. And do you know what?'

The rest of the crowd stepped out of the way and revealed another woman.

'You were right.'

Chapter 34

She searched Edward's face for permission, although in truth, it was only to buy herself another moment, to take in this woman with brief glances, this beautiful woman she hadn't seen in twenty long years, for if she didn't take her in short spurts, her heart would burst.

Edward nodded, encouraging her to approach.

Cupping her hands to her mouth, she flinched with the pain. Pain was good though, for it meant that this was real, not an observation like a dream would be. It meant she was definitely awake.

'Is it really you?'

Her mother stepped towards her, and Victoria was out of her seat, vaulting up to the stage until she was once more in her arms. How could she forget her mother's smell, or how soft her hair was? She never got the chance to experience how slight her mother's body felt in her adult arms, but she took it in now, every new and old sensation. When they broke away, she saw her mother wore the jumper, Vicky's favourite, the one she could never find after she died and believed her father purposely got rid of.

'There's so much I need to say.'

Her mother smoothed her hair, and Victoria, happily regressed, moved into her touch like a child.

'No need. I already know everything there is to know, I always have.'

'But I need to say sorry for—'

Her mother tipped her chin. 'You don't need to apologise for anything. I know you, Victoria. Every desire, every fear, every shame, all your so-called flaws, your heartbreak, I already know. What is in your heart, what occupies your thoughts, what wakes you at night, drives you out of bed, I already know, so there is nothing you need to say. It is you that needs something from me, and I want you to listen.'

Her mother picked up her injured hand and as she did, a warm sensation prickled in Vicky's palm. The yellowed bruises turned a dark-brown, then faded to a lighter shade. Her skin tingled, as the bruise shrank. The nerve endings from the tips of her fingers to her elbow grew hot, hotter, until they burned. The marks reduced until they disappeared. Until the pain was gone. Her hand was completely healed.

'Each day, I live through you. I couldn't appear, couldn't move things, couldn't force an outcome, even though I tried. We can send signs, or suggest gentle ideas, and, if you are ready to receive, you do. Christian was my gift. Christian was the way I could give back. Remember the urge to get on the bus? And that gust of wind that you always wondered about? That you said came out of nowhere, sending that money out of your hand and into Christian's lap?'

'You?'

Her mother placed her hand on Victoria's heart. 'Me.'

This time, when they embraced, she wrapped her arms around her until she was in danger of breaking ribs.

'I need you to return,' her mother whispered into her ear.

She broke away. 'Return?'

'Return to the girl who wasn't afraid to talk to someone on a bus. Who wasn't afraid to take a chance on someone, or share a bed, or laugh.'

'I'm not afraid.'

And then she was back again. In her room. Next to Edward. He spoke as if it was him she was talking to all along.

'No. That you're not. Afraid isn't a word I'd call you. Determined is.

And when our girl is determined, nothing else can win. Everything is going to work out. There's no need to worry at all, everything works out exactly as it's meant in the end. Everyone on earth is living on borrowed time, some are just more aware of it than others. Stop hiding. Stop letting fear of living kill you slowly. Live, Victoria. Do you know what we would give to spend more time here?'

They sat together then, needing no words for a long time. In the early hours of the morning before the darkness turned, when the sun hadn't yet risen, but the glow from it took the edge off the deep black, Vicky felt the slip of sleep. She tried everything to keep her eyes open, to stay present for Edward, but she was fighting what she couldn't avoid. She let herself close her eyes for a second. When she flicked them open, Edward was still there, watching.

'It's fine, go to sleep. I'll be here. There's no point talking now, you need rest.'

'But you will leave.'

'Everything that needs to be said will be said. Just rest your head now and I'll watch over you.'

'You won't sleep?'

'Go on, now rest.'

She fell asleep instantly.

Edward waited until her breathing shallowed then covered her with a blanket. He smiled at his granddaughter as she wriggled into it, then, noticing the sky brightening, he turned the lock on the backdoor and sat in a wicker chair.

'Make it a good one,' he whispered.

He puffed up pillows and settled down and waited for the day to erupt in front of him and when it did, Edward felt the full joy in the breaking, in the opening up of the dawn, shaking his head at the sight. It felt better than it ever had when he was alive. For now he was aware of what it felt like to lose it. Hours passed outside, with no need for a blanket, despite the biting wind and November chill, for the dead don't feel the cold. Gifted with the chance to experience it all again, he let the other senses seep back. The world was a pulsing, energetic thing. He sat in awe of the tiny droplets of dew on the grass and leaves. Listening to the birdsong in the distance and the sound of life waking up. He watched his breath fog in front of his face and chuckled. Oh, to have breath once again! To have a body and a beating heart. He could still feel the imprint of Victoria's hug. The prickle of her touch still lingered; a hug he had waited all her life for and had never imagined experiencing on earth.

To feel another human, soft skin and feathery hair and pulsing, vibrant energy condensed into a shell of pure aliveness was a joy. The knowledge that it was only temporary, that these sensations were all only on loan, made the present more beautiful.

To be given one more day was everything.

And he would do everything in his power to help Victoria discover that too.

Chapter 35

When she woke, it wasn't with a gasp or because of any banshee wailing. Victoria woke one eye at a time, followed by a smile. It was the wind that woke her, still blowing its angry breath, loud enough to wonder how it was possible for her to sleep through a storm, but she had, as if someone had knocked her into unconsciousness.

Remembering Edward should be near, she sat up. No sign in the room. Leaping out of the bed, she quickly searched the house, her heart only slowed once she found him, sitting in the wicker chair. Her back yard was like a demolition site, there were branches and debris everywhere but Edward acted like he was sitting on a beach.

'Morning, granddaughter,' he said.

Victoria felt her cheeks burn. 'Morning, grandfather.'

She shuddered at the blast of wind. 'Will you come in? I know you can't eat, but my body can't function without some form of caffeine first thing.'

Edward tried to get up out of the chair, his arms wobbling from the attempt. Victoria scooped an arm through one of his and hoisted him slow enough not to hurt.

'Think I stayed too long in the one spot. Didn't know bones could creak like that,' he chuckled.

Once she took the first sip of tea, she relaxed. 'What is your plan for your last day?'

'The day will be busy. There is much for you to do.'

'Only for me?'

'Don't worry, I'll be around.'

'Good. Where do you want to start?'

'How did you leave things with Lenny?'

Victoria squirmed in her seat, realising it was a redundant question for Edward probably knew everything that had happened the night before.

'I think I may have made things worse.'

'You think?' Edward looked amused.

'Okay … I made things worse.'

'There's still time to right things though, isn't there?'

She shrugged, a heat coming over her at the thought of approaching Lenny again. It would be a first. 'I guess.'

'Knowing what you know about what happened to Christian now, does it feel easier to …'

'I don't want to replace Christian, if that's what you mean.'

'That isn't what I mean. No one can ever replace another. There is no limit with love, Victoria. No cap that says because you loved once you can never again. You will not betray Christian; you cannot betray Christian by caring for someone else.'

'Leave it now. Please.'

Edward smiled.

'The town is going to need people to help clear the roads. You will need to check on the Youth Centre, make sure everyone is safe. As a Sergeant, isn't it your duty?'

'Officially, no. It's my day off.'

'You can still go as a civilian, though, right? As a person who just wants to help. Tomorrow, when I'm gone, this town will still need you.'

She covered her face. 'This is out of my comfort zone. I normally avoid people like him.'

Edward peeled her hands away. 'How has avoiding people like him worked out for you so far?'

She lifted her shoulder in answer.

'Behind the embarrassment is fear of getting hurt. It's terrifying to trust another with your feelings. Remember what is at stake though.'

She nodded. 'Someone will die, I know. But I think you're wrong about it being Lenny. He seems too stable, too strong.'

'Sometimes the ones that seem the strongest are the people who cannot share their feelings because they don't want to seem vulnerable. You should know that. Anyway, I have never said he is the person, only that it was Lenny I saw in the sequence.'

'We are back to square one.'

'Which is why we have to do what we can to find out today.'

'There has been something niggling since you told me. One detail keeps repeating. The tattoo. Lenny definitely has one, exactly where you mentioned it, but I saw another person, Darren, with one last night. Maybe the sequence is a series of different things and even though Lenny appears, it is an order of events rather than being definitely him.'

'So, you want to go to the other man?'

'I think we have to investigate both.'

Chapter 36

Some roads were impassible, either disappearing completely by flood water or blocked by fallen trees or abandoned cars. The rain had returned and was predicted to continue until the afternoon. Knowing Knockfarraig like the back of her hand had its uses. In a treacherous cross-country journey more zig zag in direction than linear, she succeeded in reaching their destination. Every time she turned the steering wheel she shook her head in disbelief at how easy it was to do. Her hand didn't hurt at all. None of it made sense. Two days ago, if someone had tried to convince her about ghosts, she would have looked up psychiatric units for the speaker, but now, here she was, convinced her mother had visited her in a vision and healed her hand, while driving her dead grandfather around in the back of the car. It hurt her head to think about it. For once, Vicky, Victoria, whatever she was now called, was going to take the advice and just trust. Something was happening, and even though none of it could be explained or made sense, it was unfolding just the same.

The Youth Centre was a flurry of activity with a breakfast/lunch station set up. The sounds of forks scraping the hotel's china plates and chatter from people relieved to have survived the night floated up to the roof. Mercifully, Lenny was nowhere in sight. Most of the evacuees were awake and gathering their discarded bits and pieces from the night before, or eating, or cupping hot steaming mugs. Edward, happy now to have had the chance to tell her everything, was a new man around people. He walked up and offered to help dish out the food and, giving her the nod, she went to find the very person she would prefer to avoid.

One teen from the night before offered her a cup of coffee. 'I'm grand, thanks. Is Lenny around?'

The boy shook his head. 'He headed down to Main Street.'

The rain hitting the Perspex windows sounded like white noise in surround sound.

'Why? Is it bad?'

'Think so. Him and a few of the lads headed off to see if they can limit the damage.'

'All okay here?'

'Yeah, no bothers. Some people are leaving to check on their houses but most are hanging around until they get the nod it's safe.'

'Sounds like you have here covered and that's where I need to go. How are people getting home? The roads are dangerous out there.'

'Only ones who left so far got the thumbs up, as far as I know.'

The boy looked panicky, like he was worried he would get in trouble. Victoria nodded at him. 'You're doing really well. If people insist on leaving, there's nothing you can do. Just let them know I said it's dangerous out there. If they still want to leave, don't fight them.'

She waved Edward over. He reluctantly put down a plate he was just about to scoop some pancakes on.

'Lenny's down on Main Street. Fancy a drive?'

Edward glanced back at the table. 'Bit cold down there, I'd say. Maybe I could help here for an hour, give you and Lenny a chance to talk without an old man hanging off you?'

'Only for an hour?'

'Hour at the most.'

'Fine.'

For a man who'd came looking for her, he kept making her leave him.

Chapter 37

Four streets away from Main Street, houses were ankle deep in water. The sea took anything beyond that. She parked the car and walked towards the worst of it, armed with her trusty backpack and waterproofed gear from head to toe. Quickly it became deeper, every couple of steps rising another centimetre on her trouser leg. So she was glad now she'd changed into her waterproof pants and boots, although it wouldn't be long before the wet got in. The rain at least had stopped again, but the wind was still relentless. Not sure where the worst of it was, she followed the sounds and soon enough came upon people. By Cobalt Street, a slip road that ran onto Main, it was up to her knee. Main Street was no longer a street but a swimming pool. The waves had taken over and were now slamming into buildings.

Before the flooded area, a group of about twenty men surrounded Lenny, huddled in patches on the same mission. Further in the distance, past the flooded street, near a dry area on the incline of the hill, she could see fire engines. The firefighters used to working with water in a different capacity this time used their hoses to suck instead of soak.

Before Lenny noticed her, she watched him at work. Thigh deep, he waded from a house with a screaming child over one shoulder. He kept going until he reached a car beside one of the fire engines, with a woman holding the door open. His hood had fallen from his head, his long hair stuck to his face like a veil, yet he didn't stop moving to push it away.

Once the child was safe, he closed the door and ran back to the building, then seconds later, emerged with another smaller child, he kept his mouth to the child's ear, his lips moving and she could imagine his soft voice, reassuring. Head down, he kept going, and she understood then Lenny was a fighter through and through.

She went to step further into the water but hesitated. Her breath hitched. Water was her weakness. Water had taken everything away. Lenny ran into another building, no hesitation from him. If she wanted to help, if she wanted to talk to him, if she wanted to mend what she had tried to sabotage, she needed to take a step.

There was nothing else to do but wade.

Chapter 38

The water chilled the bones in her feet in an instant. Her fabric stuck to her skin and added weight to her movement, slowing her down, yet she kept on going.

Passing the men without a glance, there was only one person she set out to talk to and didn't stop until she reached him. By then she was hip deep in water. Deciding against calling his name and given him the opportunity to ignore her, she placed a hand on Lenny's soaked back. He turned around, and, instead of him being the one surprised, gave her a start with his smile.

Avoiding looking at him, she glanced over at the waves as they crashed into the wall. The beach now hidden; the sea overspill only added to the flood in front. The only piece of dry land was on the hill, to the left of them. Lenny was still looking at her when she looked back. This time she couldn't help but return the smile. His face was easy to smile at.

'I know Knockfarraig's small but if you wanted to avoid me you could've managed it for at least a couple of days.'

'Storms will force you into dangerous situations when you're a Garda.'

'Am I dangerous?'

'The deadliest kind.'

'How's the hand?'

Thinking the conversation surreal in the circumstances, she held it out. 'Couldn't be better.'

Icy wet hands cupped hers. 'Looks good, better than good, it looks like you never even hurt it. Good. I've been thinking about that hand.'

'Just the hand?' She dared to look at him. His thumb brushed her skin.

'And its attachments.'

She pulled her hand away.

'Lenny, look, I just wanted to explain.'

He took a step back. 'No need, honestly. Let's just do what needs to be done and we can talk later, if you want.'

'Sounds good.'

There was that dimple, cute enough to make her blush.

There it was. The truth, her truth. No matter how much she wanted it to be different. In the middle of a storm, with water hip-deep, with half her mind on her dead grandfather while planning to evacuate a town, no matter how much she didn't want to admit it, all she wanted to do was to kiss the man standing in front of her.

Before she had time to act, or tell him, she caught a flicker of movement, behind Lenny, much further away. At first, she thought it was a piece of debris – some clothing item swept away from an apartment or shop. But then she saw it, a clear, definite hand. She gasped. Lenny shifted, following her gaze, then stepped away from her, nearer the shape. As soon as he realised what he was looking at he was off, he didn't hesitate. Not like her. She reached for him, just as he leaped through the water.

'Lenny don't, it's too dangerous.'

Whether he heard her or not, he didn't pay her any attention. Lenny dived into the shallow water when he realised it was quicker to swim than wade. The hand was joined by a head now, bobbing out to the sea rather than in the safety of the flood water. The violent current dragged the person under. Victoria waded, then stopped, listening to her instinct. To swim blindly to the drowning person would only result in both of them being sucked into the swirling black waters. It was clear to her now.

Lenny was swimming towards his death. Forget the tree, forget saving his life tomorrow, for Lenny wouldn't survive another ten minutes in that current. No one else had noticed the person bobbing in the water. Instead of following Lenny, Victoria turned left, pushing through the water, trotting, all the time shouting, roaring to the firemen near the hill, while waving to get their attention.

Every second unnoticed was a second less of breath when the waves hit. Every second Lenny moved away was another second needed to catch up. Not one more piece of time could pass without action, for every second counts when someone you care about might die.

Chapter 39

By the time she reached close enough to the firemen for them to notice her clamouring for their attention, Lenny had disappeared from view. Strapping lads, distracted by their own task until they followed the direction of her pointed finger. A flash again of skin in water and the men were on it, springing into action and grabbing what they needed, then wading through the sea with their ladder till the ground turned from hard concrete to spongy sand. Men in a crisis are quick to dive in. Victoria knew the hard way how much visibility is lost in the water.

The firemen stood in tandem, keeping each other in place, pulling out the ladder further. One edged the truck back, getting as near as he could. The ladder faced the wrong way. Lenny could not see it, couldn't get to it even if he tried. The men searched the water with desperate strokes in random directions but could not find Lenny or the other person. In the wind her screams meant nothing.

What should I do?

The question was posed to Edward but then she changed it, changed the direction of who to ask.

What should I do?

At first, she thought there weren't enough seconds to wait for an answer. Time was not a commodity to waste. But when the answer came, clear and in her own voice, the few seconds of attention brought a reward.

Because then she knew what she needed to do.
And with that she ran away from them all.

Chapter 40

Go higher.

While men waded in, a woman used her eyes to help them see. As she left the water and stepped on dry land, the wet material in her clothes dragged at her skin, holding her back, as if trying to return her to the water. She pumped her legs harder, ignoring the chafe as it ripped the surface of epidermis, pulling on the scar tissue on her thigh. Another reminder of how dangerous her last collision with water was. Reminding her of what more she could lose if she didn't act. Skin would heal, and her multitude of scars were a map of suffering long accepted, adding another one wouldn't matter. Lenny was what mattered. She couldn't lose another to the water.

Up higher, the wind enveloped her ears, sounding like a hundred spirits all chanting or screaming. On the hill, it was easier to decipher where the waves met floodwater. From above she could see the currents, the firemen, the ladders, the debris. Best of all, she could see Lenny. A hand went to her chest to stop it from beating out of the bones that surrounded it.

He was alive.

He had reached the figure and had done everything right, the person lay in recovery mode, on his or her back, with Lenny behind, his head bobbing up and down in the water from his legs pumping underneath. Perfect execution, in a pool he would have saved the person in minutes.

In the sea though, it wasn't enough. The waves blasted them from behind and front. There was no way Lenny could avoid swallowing water, so it was only a matter of seconds before he would disorientate, would start to go under. Once that happened, the rescuer would need rescuing too and the person he was saving, if still conscious, would start to panic. Never good. Someone alert will fight to the death for their last breath, when panic sets in they will claw and use a head, any head, as a buoy. They will climb on a body until the hero drowns. From fear, they will kill, when all they need to do is float.

At the apex of the hill, she found the first buoy. The rope was long, long enough to reach. She ran to the edge of the cliff. The waves did their best to climb up and hit her.

It was important to judge it right. One shot. The wind would make it difficult, send the rope in the entirely different direction if she didn't time it within a gap of wind. Even if it did send it a little off, as long as she held onto the rope she could steer it to the correct position. She tried to judge the strength of the wind, and threw well wide, landing ten feet away. Lenny didn't notice her efforts. Lenny was fighting for his life.

She rummaged in her backpack until she found the industrial strength speakerphone and torch. *I knew I'd need ye one day.* Adjusting the volume to the maximum, she called his name. Despite the whistling and hums from the wind, her voice cut right through. She called his name, called instructions over and over.

'To your left, Lenny. Life buoy to your left, Lenny.'

A slight jerk from his head. Had he heard?

She repeated. 'Life buoy to your left, Lenny.'

Whether she was hallucinating or just from her imagination, she thought she saw a shift in his direction.

'Life buoy to your left, Lenny.'

And then he was moving, bobbing in the direction of the buoy.

'Nearly there Lenny. About eight feet away. Keep going!'

She didn't add how impossible it was to swim one foot when you are in a current. Now that Lenny was alerted to the rope, she concentrated on edging it closer shifting the rope a little, nearing it to him, afraid in case it caught a gust and lifted in the opposite direction.

'An inch at a time is better than a metre the other way,' she whispered.

Inch by inch the two of them closed the gap. Lenny's fingers stretched. The distance between Lenny and the buoy, only measured about a hand. Then Lenny disappeared under.

Come on Lenny. The life buoy is just there. Keep going.

She held her breath. Clung to the rope.

Please Lenny, keep going.

His head bobbed, then a flash of skin. She let out her own breath knowing he could too.

With one hand she found the torch and shone it just in front of his face, a little distance from the buoy.

'Follow the light, Lenny!'

One head bob, two, three and his fingers just missed the buoy.

Come on, Lenny, one more push.

A wave hit his face and Lenny went under.

Chapter 41

Time split in two. Once again, she was on the side of the embankment searching for Christian while at the same time watching Lenny drown. Two men she cared for. One was lost. One still here.

Edward don't let me lose him too.

As soon as she thought it, she knew it wasn't Edward's choice. It wasn't Edward directing any of it. None of them were. She was a slave to the water again. To the black, violent sea.

'Haven't you taken enough? You want to take two men I care for now, is it?' she screamed without the speaker phone.

As soon as the words were out, she understood they weren't fair. The sea would do what it always would. They were the ones invading its space, unnaturally residing in a place never meant for them to live. The currents did what the world needed, to restore, to keep the earth in balance. It was them that shouldn't try to take from it.

I should not have been afraid, for you were never my enemy. You didn't drown Christian; he died before he hit the water. For a reason I do not understand, you didn't take me even though I offered myself to you. Give Lenny safe passage also. Please.

Her body stilled and a strange calm ran through her. While chaos still surrounded, Victoria stared at the buoy, willing it, willing him to reach it. Her eyes never left it until she saw a hand wrap around.

Once his hand locked on, Victoria flashed the torch on Lenny. Using morse code she signalled for SOS.

'Follow the light! Follow the light!' she shouted through the speaker phone.

The firemen shifted the direction of the ladder.

Within seconds, they reached Lenny with the ladder. It all happened quickly after that, once he could cling on to the ladder, the firemen could reel the ladder in.

Hot tears warmed her frosty face. She allowed herself that release, allowed herself to cry while still at a distance away. By the time she reached the makeshift first-aid station the warm tears had dried. Her face icy cold again. Instead of relief, every foot closer to Lenny, the hotter Victoria's blood boiled.

She checked on the other person first. A man, Tony Cummins, a volunteer trying to help who waded out too far to retrieve a child's toy he spotted in the water, then lost his footing on a rock below and got swept further out with the waves. In shock Tony couldn't stop crying, couldn't stop repeating, 'I thought I was going to die.'

Vicky approached a first aider. 'Will he be okay?'

'Nothing a warm cup of tea and a sleep won't fix.'

'And the other guy?' She couldn't even say his name.

'They're just checking him over but he seems the same.'

'Do you know where he is?'

The girl pointed to him.

When she reached the fire truck he was sat in she couldn't approach any closer. Knowing he was safe, as they had checked him, then covered him in foil, she paced the dry land, trying to get her heartbeat to settle to a natural rhythm. She shook too, from the adrenaline and shock, the icy wind on wet cloth from fear. Instead of running over and holding him until he was warm, or offering him a drink, or smoothing back his hair, Victoria wanted to shove him until he fell over or slap his face until it welted purple. It was unreasonable, she knew, when all she had wanted a few minutes before was for him to survive, yet now that he had, she wanted to hurt Lenny more than any criminal she had encountered, for not even the worst scumbag had made her as angry.

Through the gaps in the crowd, she saw Lenny searching for her. Forced to stay still, his head never stopped flicking from side to side, sitting up and shifting his weight to catch a look around. She understood he wanted to see her before anyone else. She wouldn't make it easy, going behind his view. As soon as he was let free, he came looking, the foil still wrapped around his shoulders, a lump around his waist as if he held something underneath. Seeing him didn't calm her, made her even madder. Before he got near, she held her fingers vertical, palm facing him. Warning him to stop.

'Have you a death wish?'

He rolled back on his heels. Dropped the smile. Not the welcome he was expecting. 'What do you mean?'

'Do you want to die, Lenny? Am I getting to know you, getting to like you.' She rubbed at her face. 'While you're, you're just looking for the best way to leave, to check out?'

This time his dimple had no effect.

'I wasn't planning on going anywhere.'

'Plans have nothing to do it. You didn't know the outcome when you dived into that water. When you were struggling for breath, you certainly didn't know it.'

'I couldn't just stand there and do nothing.'

'You could have called out for the firemen and left them do their job. Got the experts to hatch a plan but instead you made it worse, made it so two people needed to be saved from the water.'

His head dipped with a grimace. 'Sorry I disappointed you.'

'Not disappointed. Made me livid. I'm livid with you!'

She searched around for something to throw at him. Finding nothing, she used her eyes to stab him with venom.

'Instinct just kicked in.'

'That's it though, isn't it? You'll always be the guy with the instinct. Maybe this time I don't want a fucking hero.'

She went to walk away but he cut in front, blocking her path.

'I'd rather be a dead man who tried to be a hero then live the rest of my life haunted for watching a person drown while doing nothing. You're a liar if you pretend you don't spend every day trying to be one too. Being a good person wasn't on my radar for years; I told you some of this already. So, now, I spend my life making up for the hurt I caused. I'll never get there, I know that, but it feels better doing what I'm doing now than it ever did before. Life knocks us, there's none of us perfect. There's none of us without wrongdoing. Don't you think it's funny how your hunches are always right, Vicky? How when you look for the wrong in someone your success rate will always be one hundred per cent. How about you just stop looking? How about you just go for the facts?'

'Then I wouldn't be able to do my job. Digging around, my hunches, that's what solves cases.'

'Is it though?

'Yes.' Her skin burned on the back of her neck.

'See, I think there is a difference in looking at the facts and getting a feeling, 'cos that's intuition, that makes a good cop. What you're doing most of the time is assessing everyone you see, trying to find out their secrets, their flaws more like. You'll never be happy that way. How can you ever relax in anyone's company? That kind of behaviour leads to a very lonely life. What you're doing now is pushing me away.'

'Pushing you away? You're lucky I don't arrest you for endangering lives.'

He held his hands out, offering her what was in them. 'Understood.'

She took the offering, before looking at what it was. The rope. The one attached to the buoy; the one she threw to save him. A plain piece of rope, your usual type, beige in colour, thick. Exactly as Edward saw.

Her hunch was right. It wasn't Lenny that would be at the woods. The sad look Lenny was giving her was exactly as Edward described. What Edward had seen was an unfolding chain of events, not the person who was going to be the victim. Lenny, being around her, was a complete waste of time.

'Go home, Lenny.'

His free hands stayed mid-air, yet he nodded, his eyes shining with the reflection of the sea. 'As you wish.'

In her car, she banged her head against the steering wheel. 'Fuuuck.'

She drove to the Youth Centre and rushed in to find Edward in exactly the same spot she left him.

'Tracy,' she called. 'Darren been here at all?'

'No, not today.'

'I'll try him at the bar then.'

Knowing everything, Edward followed her to the car without instruction.

'We got it all wrong, Edward. We have to hurry.'

She fought to catch her breath. 'I'm messing it all up.'

'Everything will work out.'

She covered her face with her hands. 'I keep on messing up. It's like the things I want to say come out completely different.'

His hand rested on her shoulder.

'It isn't over. There is still time for you to fix it.'

'You think?'

'I know. Until your last breath nothing is over.'

Chapter 42

Even away from Main Street, the bar hadn't completely avoided the water. Although a mop and bucket would soak up the worst of the damage. The owner, Mac, pointed to the back when she asked if Darren was there, grunting his direction instead of any coherent sentence. She found him lifting his amp.

'Bringing them home?'

Darren smiled. 'Moving to dryer soil.'

As crazy as it seemed, Darren looked like he had been having a harder day than her. 'Rough night?'

Darren kept walking, struggling to hold the heavy amp. She ran to the opposite side, lifting and lightening the load. It blocked her view of him. Unable to see his facial reactions, she could only rely on the tone of his voice.

'Could say that.'

'This storm nearly got the better of us. The worst is over now, though.'

'You think?'

The way he said it nearly made her stop. She wasn't sure if he meant it as a statement rather than a question. The only other sound between them was the slosh of their feet in the water. Despite her actions to waterproof her clothes, her toes must be skinned by now, she thought.

'I saw you with that guy, Lenny, from the youth club the other day. Watch him Vic, I heard rumours.'

'Like?'

'I heard he was pretty on it a few years ago. Into drugs, into fights. Mad for the women.'

She tried to ignore the sinking feeling in her stomach. Here was her proof. She shouldn't trust Lenny.

'You sure you aren't talking about yourself there, Darr?'

'Ah, now, fighting was never my thing.'

'True.'

'Just ... watch yourself with him.'

'Don't worry, I will. How are you getting on these days?'

She cursed herself for asking when she couldn't see his reaction. He answered without hesitation.

'You know me, Vic, just keeping on.'

'You'd tell me if anything was up?'

'Yeah, yeah, sure.'

'Do you know of some woods around here? Where a river runs alongside a massive tree with a clearing?'

Darren stopped, holstered the amp with his knee, then rearranged his grip. 'There's loads of woods around these parts. Why?'

'Someone was telling me about it. Just wondering if you were planning on visiting it soon?'

He didn't move. Didn't answer either. She took his silence for surprise, wished she could see his reaction, could just picture his sheepish expression.

He carried on, and she fell in line with his steps.

'Don't tell me you're here to arrest me for illegal fishing?'

'No, not at all. Just heard it was a spot for thinking, or if you didn't want anyone to find you too soon, that's all. On a pleasant day it would be a place to go, but on a day like today, or tomorrow, in a storm like, or if someone was unhappy, best to avoid it.'

At the entrance they went sideways through the doors and, blind to where he parked, she let him lead. The back door of his van was already open. Once in, she was free again to observe.

Darren's hands went to his pockets.

'Right. No going to the woods. Got it.'

'Promise?'

'Promise.'

'Good.' She went to turn but swivelled back. 'You sure everything is okay with you, Darren?'

'All dandy,' he said, quick as a beat.

She knew then he was lying.

Chapter 43

Back in the car, Edward's smile didn't reach his eyes.

'It's time.'

She closed her eyes, hoping if she clenched them tight enough, maybe she could rewind the sentence.

He mistook her silence for hesitancy. 'Will you not say goodbye?'

'If I don't, will it stop you from going?'

'Sorry, no.'

'You only just found me.'

'Not true. I knew you before you were born. For you, it seems like only a small amount of time. We cannot go against nature's laws; they blessed us by letting me cross over but now I have to leave.'

'We have until sunset, though?'

'Which is only about an hour and a half away. It will take some time to get there and I figured you'd want to get changed again.'

'Where are we going?'

'I do not know what the place is called. I just know how to direct you there. You'll see soon enough.'

The wind left as quickly as it came. Calm once again, it had left its mark. Halloween decorations from adorned houses ended up in bushes and trees, the ones that fought and won the battle to stay upright at least. Many didn't win.

After changing out of her wet clothes, Edward instructed her to drive to a field on a road on the outskirts of town, a path she had passed nearly every day of her life. Once out of the car, Vicky followed his lead. They trudged across a field wet and boggy from the storm. Edward was slow, his old body a burden, and the sludge only made it harder. As his death occurred at a young age, Edward never slowly aged, never experienced the slow deterioration of degeneration. It was obvious how much it hurt him to walk, to move. Soon, he would no longer have to suffer. Even though she knew it was selfish, Vicky wouldn't hesitate to bring on more of his suffering if it meant she could spend longer with him. Tears prickled for what she was about to lose.

Edged by a river when they set off, the further they walked, the further away from the water they went. Until they came to a hill, where a trickle of water weaved down between some rocks.

'Help me up,' Edward said, pointing above the mound.

Vicky stepped up and held her hand out.

'Step onto that smooth stone there.'

She gripped his hand and pulled. When he stumbled, she caught him by the waist and found the strength to keep them both upright. After that, he looped her arm and step by step; they climbed the hill.

What appeared on the other side took her breath away. A waterfall flowed in front of them, small enough not to be a big deal for the tourist brochures, but beautiful enough to make her stop in wonder. In all her years in Knockfarraig, in all her explorations and discoveries, Vicky had never known this place existed.

The sky turned a deep-navy, ready for the sun to set. Massive, thick pockets of freezing fog hung above the grass. Vicky stepped back and tugged on his arm. Her whole body shivered.

'Why don't you try to stay? Maybe they won't send you back. Maybe we can have more time.'

He patted her arm, stepped forward.

'I have to, Victoria; us Fitzgerald's keep our promises.'

He straightened his crooked back, wincing while doing it. 'Anyway, this is not my life to live, not my story, for mine finished a long time ago. This is your story to write, your story to continue on.'

When she tugged at his arm again, he stopped. Then smiled.

'You already know I hate the restrictions of this old body. Those days of suffering are behind me. For you, I stepped into it again, but I want no part of this life. Death for me was beautiful, Victoria, believe me. No more pain, no more suffering. Understand, it saddened me to leave the ones I loved without a husband, without a father. And a part of me believed I missed out on so much, by never experiencing old age. Now, I understand there is no benefit to living in a decaying body except for the gift of time with your loved ones. Apart from you, mine are all gone.'

'Am I not enough?'

'Have you learnt nothing?' His jowls shook. 'Why I can't stay isn't your fault. It isn't a choice, isn't about you not being enough. Leaving has nothing to do with how much I love you. Saying goodbye isn't the same as me never being around either. If you look for signs, you will feel me, feel us. When you need us, you will feel our strength. When you call on us, our strength will give you strength. You are never alone, Victoria.'

'Then why did I feel so alone all the time then?'

'Because you didn't know better and now you do. Look, this isn't my life. What I wished for in my life, I found, even if it was only for a short time. I loved. I felt loved. What I wished for this time, I found, too. You.'

He wiped a threatening tear away from the corner of her eye. She clasped his wrist.

'What if I go with you? I don't want to suffer anymore.'

Vicky bit down on her lip, hoping to deflect the pain.

The old man tilted his head. The light from the setting sun highlighted his face, and she saw then he was fading, getting older by the minute. Yellowing skin turned the colour of English mustard, the lines of his skin deepened to thick currents, his eyes wet and rheumy. Edward was degenerating right in front of her. He touched her face with fingers cold enough to freeze skin, the scent of death wafting from the man's breath.

'This is the great secret I came to share with you; you do not have to suffer. Suffering will not make you a better person, it isn't a requirement for heaven. It is a choice. You cannot erase or change the suffering that already happened in your life, but what you haven't understood, what most people don't understand, is that you choose to suffer. There is no reason to carry it around afterwards. Yet people spend years, decades lugging around the pain. You can stop at any moment; you don't have to die to do that. From now on, just choose different choices. It isn't your time to go, there is too much for you to do here yet. Your story isn't over.'

'I don't know where to even start.'

'Start by following the first suggestion, by helping the person in the woods. Remember what we spoke about. There are lessons from the last few days that will only make sense when they reveal themselves.'

'Is it Lenny, or Darren, or someone I've missed?'

'I don't know.'

'If it's not them, how will I find out in time? How will I find the woods?'

Edward rubbed her arm. 'You need to figure out the person by yourself. I'm sorry, I don't know that answer. The woods I can help you with. It is near, just follow the river north. When you reach the oak tree with a blue fairy-door glued onto its trunk, that will signify the start of the trek. Take a right and then go straight. It will get quite dense in parts where you may think you have gone off track, but listen to your instincts, it will guide you to where you have to be.'

'All the people you spoke about in your stories are dead. You're leaving me alone again. There's no one here who loves me, no one here I love, no one I'm close to.'

Edward tugged on her sleeve.

'Maybe you need to do something about that. To live a life without someone close, without someone to tell all your stories to, or listen to on a bad day, or touch, would be such a shame. You'll have plenty time to catch up with the rest of us in eternity. And you are wrong. There are people who love you. Your father for one.'

'My father? He will leave me as well soon.'

Edward pursed his lips. 'Not soon enough, I'm afraid. His body is still strong. When the mind degenerates, it is hard to separate what they once were with what they are now. Parts of your father are already with us. Go to him. He will tell you what you need to hear. He will have some answers.'

'My father doesn't even know who I am.'

'That's why he will talk. If he thinks he's talking to a stranger, he won't be afraid to tell you the truth. Try it, Victoria, he might surprise you.'

'Can you tell me anything about what to expect? I mean ... what's over there? Is it better? Or is it nothingness, like a long sleep?'

He closed his eyes.

'Words cannot explain it, only experience.'

'Is it worth it, though?'

He smiled.

'A life lived with love is worth anything, even death. If I hadn't loved, well, I can't answer that.'

'I want to be happy, like you.'

He stroked her face. 'You do not have to die to be happy. Happiness is also a choice. This is what you should know; we share your joy, and when joy is far away, we are with you on your darkest days. All your loved ones that passed on follow you, cheer you on, so you are never alone. The next time you smile, the next time you cry, remember we are there.'

He waved his hands in the air. 'Look around you, Victoria. Death doesn't have to be ugly. Look at the leaves, the bright reds and oranges and purple. The darker days starve the leaf of chlorophyll, forcing the green to break down. Pushing the carotene to the front, appearing more dominant, producing that beautiful orange or anthocyanin for the reds. When we see that colour, we don't think of the decay, we only see the beauty. All the seasons hold the power to remind us to pause.'

They watched the sun descend.

'Time to go,' Edward said.

Her throat constricted.

'How will I hear you? How will I get to speak to you if I need you?'

'Get silent. Or rather, allow silence in. If you make it a habit, if you sit in silence, or just notice the sounds around, you give space for our messages to come.'

They hugged one last time. Victoria's chest tightened, her throat constricting until she thought it was possible for a heart to burst from sadness. Edward regarded her, then smiled.

'Live for us. Please.'

Victoria tried to think of a way to make him stay, to prove she was worth staying for, to keep him with her, but he was already fading, his skin becoming separate atoms, almost pixelating, becoming formless.

Edward let go, then stepped into the water, wading in, never stopping. Even though the water must have reached arctic levels, he never shuddered, never slowed, kept going, one foot in front of the other. With each step, his profile changed. The loose clothes stretched taunt from his widening shoulders; his hair darkened. Edward grew taller, straighter. Younger. Halfway to the waterfall, he turned back. The same man who flashed before her in her house stood again. A man about her age, dressed in a uniform with dark hair, the spitting image of her father. The wrinkles smoothed out then disappeared, the limp gone, the blush returned to his cheeks. He saluted her once, and after she returned the salute, her hand went automatically to her chest because she had to hold it there, hold it in case her heart followed him.

'I love you, Grandad,' she whispered, knowing even though he was too far away, he would still hear.

And then Edward shrunk smaller, until the clothes swamped his frame, and with each step the years rewound, reduced his body in size and age, younger and younger until he reached the waterfall. Once more, he turned, this time a boy about nine years old, the spitting image of herself at that age, his wave energetic and full of mischief. And then he was gone. Vicky was unsure whether he stepped into the waterfall or disappeared.

She stared at the water for a long time, waiting for what she didn't know. Not for Edward, for he wouldn't return. Stuck to the spot, she didn't know what to do next, so she waited for something to force her to disembark. Edward's clothes that were once Christian's floated on the top of the water. Both men lost to her once more. Here was her leaving sign. Edward was gone, Christian was gone, and there was no more reason to stay.

Chapter 44

Knowing she was never alone had an unprepared-for outcome. She cast a glance over her house with a stranger's eye. There was not one thing in the place that was of sentimental value. Every object, seat or wall was boring and colourless. When had she stopped collecting memories? When had she stopped allowing herself personal gifts or letting in beautiful things?

It was only 6pm.

One night before her mission in the woods. One night to absorb the lessons Edward left. There was plenty more cleaning up to do in the town, but for once, this time, she would leave someone else take the reins.

Edward had touched every aspect of her life. Reminders of him were everywhere. About to bite into two stale pieces of bread and cheese, she deposited them in the bin.

The dead can't taste.

Since Christian's death, she hadn't used an oven once. It was their thing – concocting meals from whatever was in the fridge, each one trying to best the other with their elaborate creation, turning the music up, and standing shoulder to shoulder chopping, slicing, stirring while informing each other on their daily anecdotes. Since his death, she ate on automatic, blending hot water with a packet or shoving some barely glanced-at meal into the microwave.

No more.

After scrubbing her dusty pans, she prepared dinner, taking her time to add long forgotten ingredients like frozen garlic, a packet of unopened parmesan. It was only bland pasta until a twist of pepper, a knob of butter, awakened it. Her salivary glands swooned.

Staying on the course of focusing on the senses, she drove to the late-night store to buy herself satin sheets. How many times had she passed them and swooned at the touch, then scoffed at the expense and moved on? What was the point of her savings if she never spent on herself? Who the hell was she going to give it to? She had no children, no relatives as such, no reason to save it. In the shop, she filled up the shopping trolley with colourful cushions and throws, scented candles delicious enough to tempt you to take a bite rather than sniff and bright flowers to fill new vases.

A thrill ran through her as she handed her credit card over and she knew then it was Edward's way of letting her know he approved.

In the care home, she sat next to the man who she visited once a week for the last few years, the same man she had found impossible to live with when she was younger. Her father didn't acknowledge her when she greeted him, didn't look her way or even move. Just continued to stare out the window. It was quite a feat; she hadn't even seen him blink.

'Here goes nothing,' she said under her breath.

'Did you know you are the reason I became a Sergeant? Because of you, I craved structure, wanted rules, wanted to know that when people wrong others, they have to answer to someone. When the answers from the source never came from you, I wanted to enforce others who suffered did get an answer. I needed to know I could right some wrongs.'

He turned as if only noticing there was someone in the room. 'My daughter wants to be a Garda.'

Instead of correcting him like she always did, she stopped. It wouldn't make any difference, would only embarrass him, only make him retreat under whatever blanket of memory he hid under. Remembering Edward's advice, she played along. 'Oh yeah? How old is she?'

'Five.' His eyes shone with alertness, which was a rare sight. 'She's some live wire. Always asking questions, always wanting to change the world.'

Talking about his daughter, her father's features changed. He made eye contact with her, he acted more present than she had seen in years.

He leaned closer, as if about to tell her a secret. 'You know, people make out parenting is hard, but I tell you, Vicky makes it easy.'

He smiled at her, with no recognition, no recollection whatsoever.

'Makes what easy?'

'To love that girl.'

Those words twisted something inside Vicky. Hardened her again. 'Would you consider yourself a good parent, then?'

He didn't respond to the sarcastic edge, didn't seem to even notice.

'Kids are easy to love. What's hard is putting aside your mess, loving someone when everyone you trusted with your love hurt you.' He wiggled his finger. 'Learning to love, now that's the kicker. In fairness, her mother tried to get through, but I fought her every step of the way.'

He stopped mid-sentence. For a second, she thought she had lost him to his illness again. 'Sometimes, when I see my little girl, I have to look away because deep down, I know I'm going to mess her up. I'll only disappoint her.'

He stared off in the distance and Vicky was afraid to move in case it distracted him from continuing. He cleared his throat and when he flicked his eyes in her direction, it was as if Edward had somehow taken over her father's body and was speaking again. Yet, it was still her father, his voice, his mannerisms, the man she remembered, who spoke next.

'We learn our parents' ways. Even if we don't want to. As much as we might want to run away, or fight against what they were, they find us, no matter how much we hide, or how far we go they are present in the blood that runs through our veins. We learn their beliefs, their ways. Inherit their hurts, navigate through the fresh pain they dish out. Until their pain becomes a part of our life. Until it is us.'

He bit down on his lip.

'I won't do that to my daughter, won't hurt her like my father hurt me. He wasn't there and the love for him had nowhere to go when he died and I swear I won't let her hurt like that. I'll always be around, be near, I'll never move away.'

He tapped the air. 'At a distance. Love hurts too much when you lose them. I can't risk it. If anything happened, I can't.'

His fingers flicked at the space in front. 'When she's just playing, messing around like, running or jumping, my head goes to a million things that could happen, a ton of different disasters and I can't cope with the fear; if anything was to happen, my heart wouldn't keep going. I don't know what to do with it. It wrecks my head.' He caught sight of her then, as if only just noticing her. 'Sorry, did I say something to upset you?'

She wiped at her eyes, shaking her head. 'Not at all, the opposite, actually. Your words make sense, they make me understand. You're right; we learn our parents' ways. Until they are our ways too. I have kept people at a distance, just like you. Avoided any possibility of pain. Since I met Edward, he showed me what I've missed. He showed me life isn't special without love.'

Her father nodded in agreement, then grinned. Victoria's breath hitched, for in that moment, he was in total agreement with what she said. In that moment, her father loved her, loved his little girl.

'Edward, you say? Same name as my father.'

'Really? It's a lovely name, a kind name.'

'Yes, I guess it is.'

And then his eyebrows knotted together. He flicked his eyes from one side of the room to the other, the moment gone, the discomfort setting in, the memory fading, the proof of his awareness leaving.

'Love is worth the hurt,' she whispered.

Chapter 45

On the second morning of November, she rose while still dark and dressed in her uniform, even though it was her day off. It was comforting for the town on a day like this, when destruction surrounded, a Garda in uniform could reassure without words. She stopped at a shop and bought a newspaper. The headline in the newspaper was titled: Murderer will rot.

Despite the seriousness of the article, she smiled. Because it was exactly as Edward said it would be.

Trust me, Victoria.

It took some time to find the woods while searching in the dark. Twice she wondered if she was walking in the wrong direction. When she spotted the oak tree though, it was undeniable as the one Edward described: a lone tree in the middle of a field, its branches fanned out, breathtaking and regal, with a little blue fairy-door on its trunk. After that, the place in the woods was exactly where Edward directed. Before dawn she arrived, consoled when there was no one yet there. Exactly like Edward described in his story, the woods were a peaceful place, the only sounds coming from the river, from the sway of that big, inviting tree.

After a while of no action, doubt set in that it was the wrong spot, that she was wasting the opportunity to help. Then she remembered the plaque. As the day brightened, she searched the ground. Her fingers touched uneven mud, loose stones, burrowing insects and clumps of grass and then, sure enough, for she never doubted Edward's description, only her sense of direction, she found the headstone peeking up through the weeds. Once cleared and free again, she ran her fingers along the indent, tracing the names of her ancestors, then spoke in as close to a prayer as she could.

'Help me say the right thing to whoever turns up.'

Once she explored every inch, she moved to the snug of the tree. After getting comfortable, she watched the river while nibbling on the sandwich she purchased with the paper. Clear and shallow enough in one section to see underneath, one large stone broke the surface, causing a ripple in the stream. It disrupted the flow, forcing the water to change course around it in order to carry on. Like Edward said, if the water stayed rigid, it could not go further, only slap against the stone then fall backwards. Being rigid caused problems. The fact that water stayed fluid enabled it to sidestep the blockage, move around with ease and, even though its course calibrated, the journey did not stop. How long had she turned rigid? How long had she stopped being fluid? Christian's death was the beginning. That night had stripped her, ripped his life, his love away, and she had lain her own life down in offering, choosing to suffer. For what? It didn't help Christian. It didn't bring him back. And then it hit her. Why she had felt such sadness since Edward left because as much as she missed the old man, as much as she came to love him in twenty-four hours, his appearance represented hope, gave her the faith that Christian could, might, return too. On that stage, she had scoured the line for one person, before even her mother. In her life, Christian had been the forefront, the grounding, the one to make her smile when all around her was serious, her only love, the only man who had shown her that love didn't have to hurt and yet despite all his promises, all his assurances, he still had. Once he died, he had hurt her more than anyone could ever hurt her alive. Christian was the ghost that always followed.

After that, she didn't notice the river or the sky or gravestones or blades of grass, all the edges blurred until all she could see was within, was the life she shared with Christian. She replayed the images of their relationship, attempting everything in her power to conjure him up, because if any place could do it, it was this magical place.

'Bring him back,' she whispered. 'Give me one day,' she said louder.

'One day, that's all I ask,' she shouted.

She stood, then screamed with all the air in her lungs. 'I want one more day. Do it now! Right now, bring him to me.'

Nobody answered. The only sounds were from the river still flowing.

'Please. Bring him to me.'

Slumping down along the trunk of the smooth tree, something inside her finally broke. She had cried for Christian many times since he died, too many times to count, but this time was different, because she wanted the tears to flow at the same rate as the river beside her moved. This time, though, she couldn't; it was as if there were no more tears left. It was as if Edward's visit dried up the possibility. Instead, she imagined letting them go as if they streamed down her skin, until they became as liquid as the water. The thought loosened all her knotted muscles, all the resentment she held inside. All the rigidity she had built up in her body softened. And then she did something so unlike her, so crazy, so far from the person she allowed herself to be. Victoria howled at the sky. Like a wolf calling to the night. She let her lungs open wide until the sound didn't need to voice her pain any longer. Her fingers clawed the dirt, raking the ground where her great grandfather bled deep, then fertilised the roots of the tree below. She howled until she ran out of breath, then did it again. No one could hear. Just her and her pain. She howled until she didn't need to anymore, until it was easy to quieten and calm. Until she was ready to meet the person by the tree.

Chapter 46

All day she stayed, all afternoon she waited. No crackle of leaves sounded, no parting of weeds or stirring of grass. Edward's premonition took place in the daylight, so by sunset it would be over. Vicky retraced her steps, replayed conversations, remembered the people she had met over the last few days. Had she saved the person already? Had something she said changed the outcome, changed where the person would go? With a sickening thud, she wondered if she had only changed the place with her actions. Was someone somewhere else doing what she planned to save them from? Was it Lenny after all? What if he was self-harming somewhere else? She had been livid with him for diving into the water. Completely, irrationally angry. She believed then it was because of his recklessness, for his complete lack of care for his life. A pain surged in her chest, because even keeping him at bay, staying angry couldn't take away the pain of what it would feel like to lose him. In a matter of days, it already hurt. How much would it hurt if she loved him, only to lose him later? Was she willing to take the chance?

For the rest of her life, she would love Christian. But loving Christian didn't mean she couldn't find a place for Lenny. It wasn't cheating or dismissing what they had before. Could she open her heart again? It was a terrifying contemplation. It felt like a betrayal to imagine a relationship with Lenny.

Christian, would you think the same?

She finally asked him, and then she waited. It didn't take long for an answer to come.

Every detail of him was in front of her. The scar under his lip from missing the rung of a treehouse as a child. His hair as she liked it best, long on top, shorter on the sides. Those deep-blue eyes, with flecks of minuscule green. She wanted to cry with happiness. She wanted it to be real. His fingers laced through hers. Kissing each fingertip. His nails bitten to skin, his only vice he joked. It's nerve-wracking living with you, Vic, he used to say. There was always laughter around him.

'What would I do without you?' she asked him one day as they lay in bed.

'You'd forget about me before I was even out the door.'

She tapped him on the chest. 'How dare you. I'd fall apart. I wouldn't go on.'

The gravity of her sentence forced her to curl into a ball. He cupped his body around. Warm stomach on her back.

'I know you would. But then you wouldn't.'

'Don't say that, Christian, you're upsetting me.'

'I'm not meaning to. Just listen. If we were to ever part, you would, for a while you would fall apart. But then, you'd piece together. You'd find a way. I'd want you to.'

'What? You'd be happy if I met someone else. Marry some guy from down the road?'

He spoke in kisses. His voice vibrated against her skin.

'Why not? A soulmate doesn't have to stay forever.'

'I'd haunt you if it was me.'

She twitched next to him, still annoyed. 'I would never forget you, never replace you.'

His breath tickled her ear. 'Loving someone else wouldn't mean you love me less.'

As the memory disappeared, she allowed herself to cry.

Christian loved her with every part of him: soul, body, mind. He had lived his life full of love, taught her how to open hers, showed her how to trust, showed her what kindness was like. A man like that would want her to stay kind, stay loving, stay open. Would he want her to close herself off from what he loved about life?

No.

In her heart, she knew. Christian would want her to be happy; that was the truth. Hadn't Edward said this? That her loved ones wanted him to step in, to teach her to be more open, to not be afraid of love.

Love is worth the hurt.

When Edward transported her to the cinema, Lenny stood in that line of people she helped. *Had* helped. He wasn't the one needing saving here. There wasn't anyone doing what Edward had seen somewhere else. It was this place. Otherwise, what had Edward come for? What would be the point of everything? The vision he'd talked about had to take place in this very setting. It had to be in the woods. Had to be today. It had to be before sunset. As the darkness crept in, so did her understanding of what it meant.

The person she needed to save was herself.

Chapter 47

The boots Edward prophesied, were hers. As the answer came, she saw what must have played out to Edward. A man from the thirties could easily mistake her boots for army-issued steel-capped ones. In his vision, it was Vicky who took the rope from the boot of her car, the same rope that had snapped from the buoy. The same rope Lenny handed over to her the day he almost drowned. Shaken, she had taken the rope and dumped it in her car, instead of throwing it away. Now she understood it was the same rope that Edward saw tied around the tree.

It was her. The person Edward saw was her. This was why it was so important to Edward – he *was* there to save his family. She could feel what that Vicky, the girl in his vision, felt. Caught up in the guilt for the way she left things with Lenny, for the stir of attraction she could no longer deny; not regretting sleeping with another man, but for allowing feelings in. Without Edward's appearance, or his advice to trust, a different chain of events would have played out. In the wrong head space, she would have barged in through those swing doors at the Youth Centre. Archie would have panicked, would have taken a shot.

Like the gift Edward gave her before of seeing what could have been, she saw it all now. The blood, the death, Lenny's death, because of course it would have been him that would have jumped out to block the others. Before anything even happened between them, Lenny's death would have broken her because she had caused something preventable, unforgivable in her eyes. After that, when the station closed, she would have nothing left to live for. The thought of returning to work in the city knowing that after a few days or months, she couldn't carry on being a Garda would have been the final sign. Missing Christian with no other family to rally around, without love or any hint of hope, she would have given up. On this day, Vicky would have ended her life.

Before Edward, this was her outcome.

'Live for us. Please.'

They were his parting words. They were what he returned to tell her.

She recalled Edward speaking about the tree.

'If the tree could talk, if it could flash all the good the person had done, it would. The person doesn't see what the river wanted to show them because they looked away too soon. If only they kept searching, it would show what they could do still if only they would live, if only they would carry on.'

As she looked at the flowing river, images flashed on the surface like a movie reel, showing how Halloween night would have gone if Edward hadn't manifested. There would have been no going home to speak to him on Samhain. There would have been no stories of her family, of what her name meant, of what suffering her family experienced before she was born. With no idea about her lineage, or about the pride she should take in representing her family.

The storm, the evacuation, the meeting Lenny, the feelings he stirred up all would still happen without Edward's presence. What would have not been there was her listening to the voice that came from behind the door that told her it swung inwards, or the conversation beforehand of how listening to the voice was important. She would have been on the wrong side of the door, watching as Archie took a fatal shot into another man she could have loved. And with his death she would have said goodbye to any chance, to any want, of going further, cementing her resolve, that loving anyone only caused them and her hurt. All that would have happened, but it didn't. And now it didn't have to.

Edward spoke about choices. Well, destiny was a choice. A choice she could make. Her life was stopped at a crossroad, and only she could choose the path. In the past, Vicky faced many crossroads. Life seemed to be made of crossroad after crossroad. Each one seemed so final at the time, as if each decision propelled her forward. And they did. But that didn't mean she couldn't go back. Couldn't reverse a decision. Closing a door didn't mean it had to stay locked. It just meant she closed it at that time. In the past, to cope, she closed her heart and mind to love. To protect. To find a way to continue to live on. But that didn't mean she had to keep that part of her closed forever. She could find a gap. She could prise the door ajar. She could choose a different road. This time, she wasn't afraid. This time she would choose love; she would choose, at least, to try again.

Victoria pushed herself up from the tree. There was no need to be there any longer. On her way, she kissed her fingertips, then tapped the headstone once, remembering how Edward had already seen this too.

'Thank you,' she whispered.

As she waded through the grass and weeds, checking for random stones that could trip and delay, the darkness crept in, and as it did, she left her own darkness with it. As she felt it leave, her body bounced and her strides grew faster until she was running, and Victoria, once Vicky, laughed because she couldn't remember the last time her body felt as light and she hurried more, rushing now, because life was too short to linger and slow down, because for once she wanted to get somewhere, get to someone and she wouldn't stop until she reached him.

Chapter 48

As she pulled into the Youth Centre, the building showed no signs of life. The lights were off; the doors padlocked shut. She drummed her fingers on the wheel. In happy ever afters, this wasn't the way it went.

Cal came round the corner of the building, his hands in his pockets.

'Lenny around?' she called out, rolling down the window.

'Nope. First Saturday he hasn't opened.'

'He didn't tell you he wouldn't?'

Cal pursed his lips, dug his hands deeper.

'Could he be inside?'

'Nah, already checked. No one's in there. Just did a lap of the place to make sure he wasn't after falling down around the side.'

'You know where he lives?'

'Nope.'

'Yeah, me neither. What about a phone number?'

The number rang out. Lenny's voice was like a breath of fresh air followed by a smack to the face when she realised it was only the messaging service. What could she say? Nothing that would sound right on the phone. She hung up.

For a moment, checking his details on the system seemed like a good idea. She thought about Lenny's wrists. About the conversations when he mentioned making many mistakes. About Edward's premonition, about him seeing Lenny's sadness. Even though she knew she had needed saving, what if she wasn't the only one? Had her actions deepened his pain? She had dismissed his feelings, believing he was strong, but what if her treatment only brought his intentions forward, only changed where he would act? What if Lenny was out there now planning to hurt himself?

Chapter 49

After no luck searching the streets of Knockfarraig, she drove to the station, cursing herself for not finding out where Lenny lived. Was it stalking if she did a background check now?

She analysed every conversation with Lenny, hoping to uncover even a fragment of information she may have overlooked.

When Darren had mentioned Lenny's previous history, instead of empowering her for being right not to trust him, it had only made her sad. It should have been exactly what she wanted – for there was the proof, there was the confirmation she couldn't trust him. Yet it only made her want to know him more. Lenny hadn't lied or pretended to be perfect. He'd already said he'd made mistakes. This truth made her want to know him more. What Darren said should have been the proof she shouldn't let her guard down – instead she recognised she wanted to be proved wrong. She was ready to trust. She was ready to want to trust.

I will not do a background check on him. I will not find out anything he isn't ready to tell me.

I will trust.

At the station, she assessed the water damage. The floor sloshed as she made her way to the cleaning closet. After ten backbreaking buckets, the water was small enough to be mopped and dried. It took her hours to clean down the station. Victoria scrubbed it until it gleamed. Her personal items only took minutes to clear in comparison: chewed biros, mint packets, hair ties, lip balm, painkillers. Pathetic remnants of a life.

Phyllis took the call well, considering Victoria couldn't tell her if the woman still had a job.

She diverted her phone and took a deep breath. Done.

Then, she wrote a sign for the door.

This station is no longer operating. Please call Ballinroe station.

Chapter 50

After a deep breath, she knocked on the door of the superintendent, rocking back when she noticed the sign on the door.

Regis Mara.

Regis. She remembered the name from her conversation with Edward but couldn't place what he told her, then smiled, remembering his constant repeat that she needed to listen.

Walking in without knocking again, she ignored the ringing phone on his desk and held out her letter of resignation like a shield; although she didn't hand it to him, for she was ready to fight for her job. On the drive, she'd planned out the meeting in every detail, sounding out the words to an empty car. Some sentences caused a prickly sensation on the underside of her arms. They were the sentences she would use.

After nodding hello, she held her free hand up to stop him from talking.

'Before you say anything, I want you to know I have listened to you about trusting people. Since you left that phone message, I've done a lot of soul searching. Before, I believed the reason I didn't want to work in the city again was because I wasn't up to it, was scared even. Now, I understand I don't want to go to the city because it feels like a backward step. I love working in Knockfarraig, love caring for every person in the town and will do anything for them, even risk my life and if you can't see how important that is, you can take my badge with my resignation.'

When he didn't respond, she lay her letter down and removed her badge, then slid them over.

He rested his hand on the badge, then stared at her for well over ten seconds. Then slid it back.

'My ears are ringing.'

She shook her head, confused.

'The abuse I'm after getting.'

He held his hand up to his ear as if talking on the phone, then in a mimicking, higher-pitched voice, 'What are we going to do without a station? Are you going to come down if we need you?' Then changed the tone to gruff. 'Garda Fitzgerald drove me home in the middle of the night when I broke down, bet you won't drive out in the rain to help me.'

Then changed his voice higher. 'Did you know she called to me every night for a month after my son died, made me tea, got me dressed? You won't do the same in that big city of yours!'

He wiped at his eyes. 'All bloody morning I'm listening to it.'

Victoria bit her lip to keep from laughing.

He sighed. 'They talk about you like the whole town would go to ruin without you leading it. Course it was Phyllis that led the pack, got all the residents to ring in. Never heard the woman say boo before today and now I have her threatening me with signed petitions. She even got the other stations onboard, got Ballinroe all riled up, complaining they're overloaded and can't cover Knockfarraig as well. None of them let me get a word in. If they had, I would have told them this storm proved how much Knockfarraig needs someone when disaster strikes. The storm proved how much you will go to help them; how brave you are.'

He picked up a piece of paper. 'Another guy, Lenny Flaherty, rang too.'

She straightened.

'To say how you helped him with Archie Costello. He explained how your quick thinking saved the lives of the people at the Youth Centre. And even though you were injured, you still transported Archie to the other station because I'd insisted on closing Knockfarraig. Also, he told me you saved him and another man from drowning. Without your quick thinking, he said, the firefighters wouldn't have found them in the water. From the sounds of it, you also successfully led a team to evacuate the buildings in danger the night of the storm.'

'What about Richie Collins?'

Mara waved his hand as if sweeping away the question.

'Richie Collins has more to worry about than suing you. He was found in Cork City trying to dispose of a body in the River Lee. Can't really do that with an arm in a cast now can he? Seems like he thought the storm was the perfect night to kill a girl and get rid of the body, except he carried her right past two officers called to investigate looting in one of the shops on the quay. Your girl will be called to testify. They are even looking into a number of girls that have gone missing since he was last released. You'll probably be commended.'

He splayed out his hands. 'Garda Fitzgerald, I don't want you to move to the city. You proved I can trust you. You proved you can put aside your doubts and trust others. That's all I ever wanted you to do. Knockfarraig is still yours if you want it.'

Chapter 51

On the drive home, she thought only of Lenny. Lenny Flaherty. In all the time she'd spoken to him, she never even asked him his surname. As if the gesture alone could make the journey faster, she leant forward. On the drive through the town, she saw the clean-up had finished. Apart from the eerie feeling from all the empty buildings, the road showed no evidence that water devoured it only a couple of days before. The sea was calm now, no raging winds, no salty burn against the skin. It shadowed her inner feelings.

Passing the bar she noticed a sign: *New Act Saturday night! DJ Aaron in the house!*

Indicating left at the crossroads, she turned for the Youth Centre but as she took it, she heard a sound, not coming from an external source. Her own voice. Checking her mirrors, her hands yanked the wheel clockwise until she drove in a circle, heading in the opposite direction.

At Darren's, the house appeared abandoned, which in itself didn't cause alarm. Used to late nights from gigging, Darren liked to sleep in. Just before she knocked, she noticed a gap between the door and the wall. Another unlocked door. The hairs on the back of her neck rose. Careful not to make a sound, she pushed it open. Boxes, three deep, lined the length of the wall in the hallway. Not alarming on their own, for Darren never struck her as a tidy person. It was the notes taped on them that caused concern.

For Delia. For Ciaran. For Mam. Another marked donations for charity.

Victoria opened the door wide. 'Darren, you in here?'

Other than a sofa, his front room was empty. Darren sat on it. Holding a gun. The ridge of it lay in his mouth.

Chapter 52

'Hear me out before you do anything,' she said.

Darren's eyes were wide in panic, his fingers moved to find the trigger. Victoria tried to breathe out the tension, hoping to help defuse the energy in the room.

'I won't stop you, if that's what you want to do. If you give me a minute and I can't change your mind, I promise you I'll leave and I won't tell anyone I was here.'

He didn't lower the gun, but his focus stayed on her, giving her the attention.

'Darr, I can't talk if you have it in your mouth, I won't be able to relax. What if I tell you a story and you're so riveted your finger twitches?'

Darren stayed where he was, unmoving.

'I won't move closer, won't try any trick leaps to get the gun away. You're just making me nervous, Darr. Just rest it beside you.'

'Only if you stay at the door,' his words barely coherent with metal in his mouth.

'I will not move.'

He didn't put the gun down but released the trigger and lowered it away from his mouth. Still, he kept it pointed at his face. All it would take to change it back was a second.

'My legs are about to go from me with the shock. I know I just promised not to move but this has been some few days and I think my body can't cope with the extra adrenaline that just kicked in. Can I get one of those boxes out in the hall and sit on it?'

Darren looked like he couldn't believe she was worried about sitting at a time like this, but after a few seconds, shrugged.

Victoria took a moment to gather her thoughts while lifting the box, then sat slow enough not to spook him.

'You know, I thought you were acting off the other day, but there were so many other distractions I didn't piece it together. I should have known when Edward showed me the tattoo. Should have known better when I mentioned the place by the trees that it would turn you off using it. I thought you were moving your gear because of the flood, but you weren't, were you?'

Darren's eyes stayed on the gun. 'Who's Edward?'

'Long story. Let's just say he's a kind of fortune teller. He warned me someone would try to take their life. What's going on, Darr?'

He didn't answer, stayed focused on the metal he held.

She glanced around the empty room. Looked further beyond to the kitchen. A multitude of tablet bottles rimmed the window. She scanned him. His long hair was greasy; he'd lost weight and there was a lump protruding from the side of his neck.

'You sick?'

This jolted him into looking at her. 'How?'

'Call it a hunch.'

She didn't say how something had niggled at her since they spoke about him fishing in the place by the woods. Or didn't add that her realisation that she was the person needing saving hadn't rung completely true either. She *had* needed saving, but if the person who took their life at the tree was her, how would she have discovered the spot without meeting Edward? Darren broke through her thoughts.

'When the cough got bad, I gave up the drink, thinking partying too hard was taking its toll. Usually when I laid off the booze and took it easy for a while, it righted. Didn't sort it this time. Went to the doc when it affected my voice. After a ton of tests, he told me it's the one to worry about. The notes don't hit right these days. Mac hasn't a clue, thinks I need to up my game, been hinting at me to take a break, so I quit. Never even smoked before. All those years in my twenties gigging, you couldn't see for the smoke, don't know if it was that, no point going over it now.'

'You didn't tell him?'

'I don't want no pity job. Who wants a singer who can't sing?'

'You're not just a singer, Darr.'

'Really? What else can I do?'

'Some would say you're a decent guitar player, too.'

'A guitar player can't keep his own Saturday night slot.'

'Just means a change of plans.'

'Won't pay the mortgage. And I'm tired of it all, Vic, you know?'

'How bad is it?'

'Which part? The cancer or the fact I'm about to lose my home?'

'Did you tell the mortgage brokers, at least?'

He shrugged. 'What's the point? I'd rather burn out than fade away, more rock and roll.'

'Please. You're giving yourself way too much credit. Dying instead of paying your mortgage isn't the same as overdosing in a pile of your own vomit.'

His focus returned to the gun. 'I knew I could rely on you for a bit of sympathy.'

'Not fair. You'd get it if I thought you were a pathetic case, but you aren't. You can't go without getting that album out. How long have you been threatening the town with the release?'

'It's there. In the box labelled for the fans.'

'Oh, I get it. You want them to play your album when you're gone, make it go viral on social media with its brilliance for the star that was lost.'

Although his eyes stayed on the gun, there was a slight quiver at the corner of his lips that could have been a smile.

'Something like that.'

'Darren, honestly, you're an idiot.'

'Kick a man when he's down then.'

'Seriously, though? How idiotic to worry about paying your mortgage when you have a whole town waiting for your music. You know they'll buy it from you.'

'Told you, I don't want their pity.'

'Darren, come on. There's been people waiting for that album for a decade. The queues go round the block for your gigs.'

'Not the last few weeks there isn't, my voice is shot, I'm telling you.'

'Well, show them what they'll miss. You getting treatment?'

He smoothed his head. 'The hair. It's my trademark.'

'Your hair's overrated.'

He laughed then, a proper belly laugh. 'Give me something, Vic.'

'Like what?'

'A break maybe?'

'Darr, I've known you since we were kids, before you were the town's big star, you used to try to scale a tree and jump down after reaching the first branch. You get no break from me. Who do you think would have cleaned up the mess you left here today? Who would have made the call to your mam and dad to tell them their boy left without giving them the chance to be there for him when he needed them? Me, that's who, so no breaks from this sucker. Fuck the house. If the banks refuse to help, you can move in to mine.'

'Seriously?'

'Couldn't be more serious. Enough friends and family have left me too young. You'll get through this, Darren, and if you don't, if it's your time to go, if you only get a short amount of time, I bet you everything I own you'll still be glad you waited to see what life had left in store for you.'

He shook his head, trying to dry his welling eyes.

'How can you be so sure?'

'Because a man taught me exactly that lesson. We have to trust.'

Chapter 53

Lenny was fiddling with some Christmas lights outside when she arrived at the Centre. He smiled when he saw her, but it was a sad smile, with none of the openness she was used to.

'How's things?' Her voice betrayed her. She'd aimed for light-hearted, instead her voice came out nervous.

His face stayed passive. He didn't bother with pleasantries, and this hurt her more than she imagined. This wouldn't be easy.

'There's a guy I was hoping to talk to you about. Billy is his name, has a penchant for hitting things with boiled eggs, amongst other things. He's been in trouble for years, but I'm hoping there's still a chance for someone to get through to him. Before, when he was only a little kid, I received some D.A. calls to the house, most he was witness to. The mum kicked the dad out eventually, but he left his mark. His mother is going through chemo and there's nothing more I can do except arrest him and I don't know, maybe, I thought, you might help him?'

Lenny didn't look up. 'Got it. Billy needs help. Pass me on his details and I'll try my best.'

'Also, I want to let you in on a secret,' she said. Lenny's concentration stayed on unravelling a knotted piece of lights.

'Every time I met someone of interest I used my position as a sergeant to do a background check.'

Lenny flinched.

'But I didn't with you. Don't get me wrong, I wanted to, and I nearly did, but then I realised everyone has a past, and everyone makes mistakes and for once, I wanted to do things differently. Lenny, I want you to tell me your history. I *want* you to tell me your story. What I've learnt over the last few days is that facts on a page don't make the person. Details like how many penalty points or even convictions don't sum up a life. They don't give a complete view of what someone is like. It is only through hearing the person's story, listening to what caused them to take each path, each crossroad, that you can understand why they made certain choices.'

Lenny continued unravelling the lights.

'And what I've learnt is those choices, those bad choices, can become part of the make-up of us or they can become the making of us. Lenny, what I'm saying is, I'm sorry for pushing you away. You scare me. I thought I needed to keep my distance from people I care about. Like my father, I thought that would save me, stop me from getting hurt. It only hurt me more. Cutting off love only caused more pain, not less. And Lenny, the truth is I want to love and I want to hear your story and I want to tell you mine. See, I understand now, I have a choice, to live or die, and instead of living a nicely balanced life, where nothing scares me, just plodding along, eating meals from a packet and going to my job finding cats and sorting the traffic, I'm ready to live again. To try living again.'

Lenny dropped the lights. Walking towards her, he wrapped her in his arms, giving her exactly what she needed. A hug.

When you hug someone, what *they* feel doesn't seep into you. If you feel nothing for the person, if you close yourself off, then the other body is just a mound of flesh, or an object, to hold. The feeling comes from you. What you feel when you hug is the key. If you feel the love and they feel the same, then the hug envelopes the emotion, for when love flows between two people, it is life changing.

'More words came out of you there than the whole time we've met.'

'See? I'm a changed woman.'

His nose nuzzled into her hair.

'No need to change. I like who you are. In future, just let me in.'

'You might need to help me.'

'Helping I'm good at.'

He pointed at the lights on the floor. 'Untangling, not so good at, I'm afraid.'

'You know it's only the start of November, right?'

He regarded her. 'Oh, don't tell me you're anti-Christmas now as well?'

'You're right. New me. Bring on the lights. See, that's where we'll make a good team. I'm an excellent untangler.'

As they both bent down to pick up the lights, their fingers touched and that was all they needed. The lights stayed on the floor. What mattered was lips and hands and beating hearts and an ache inside that she tried for too long to push down. After he led them quickly into the Centre, despite the fumbling of getting the key in the lock and closing the door, after they found their way to the couch at the back of his office, and their bodies mingled, the ache softened and became looser and looser, became fluid, building up, and instead of repressing, and pushing it away, Victoria let it take over, let it spread throughout her body, until it moved through every pore, until her nerve endings tingled and a warmth heated her whole self and an explosion of colour burst in front of her closed eyes.

This was what she wanted. Never again would she settle for microwaved meals or beige rooms. From that moment on, she wanted colour. And love, and vibrancy, and life.

Weeks later, she would understand why her life was so important. Why Edward orchestrated his time and swayed her opinion so she believed Lenny needed her help. It *was* to save his family. Or better said to save *her* family. As she waited at the place by the tree, waiting for a person to save, not knowing the person to save was her, as she lay under that tree, just as her great grandmother had lain in that same spot, both not knowing they were carrying a child inside their womb. One hundred and twenty years later, the history of the Fitzgerald clan repeated. The blood of her family ran through her veins and one day soon, it would run through her son's.

They would name him Edward.

They would marry in the place by the tree, where she walked with her pregnant belly showing proudly in her dress and a bunch of bluebells in her hand and as she passed, she would stroke the headstone and again say thank you.

And as they said their vows, Vicky held her new husband's hand, bringing the tattoo that wasn't a squiggle closer for a kiss, knowing now what it was, what it had always intended to be. The tattoo was a promise from him to never give up, to never stop seeking, to wait until he found the one who would complete his search. A declaration. Holding his hand, her wedding ring glistened in the sunshine, pointing the way to the new tattoo she now bore in the patch between her thumb and forefinger, a wedding gift for her husband, made to match his, so when they held hands, the two tattoos joined, fulfilling its destiny. Completing the shape of a heart.

The End.

Also by Natasha Karis

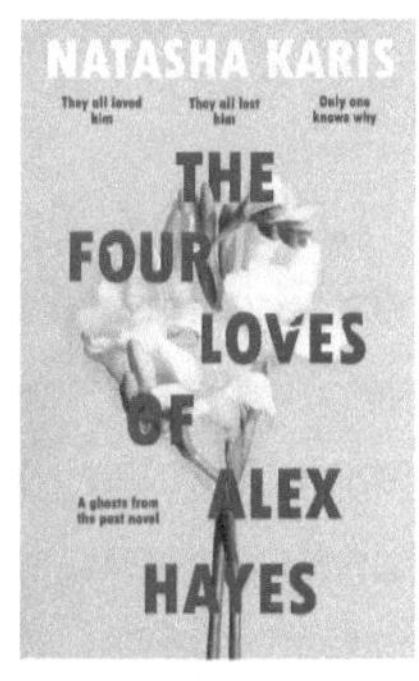

The Four Loves Of Alex Hayes

After Alex Hayes is cremated, three women and a child grieve a man they never imagined having to let go of.

But each guard a truth of their own.

As Sergeant Vicky Fitzgerald investigates the mystery surrounding Alex's final days, she begins to suspect that these women hold the answers not just to his death, but to the kind of heartbreak that changes a person forever.

Vicky, determined to discover the truth, refuses to let the case go until she reaches the shocking conclusion, pushing the women to reveal more than they ever dared to say.

An emotional family drama about hidden pasts, second chances and a love that lasts forever.

Check it out at: https://mybook.to/thefourloves

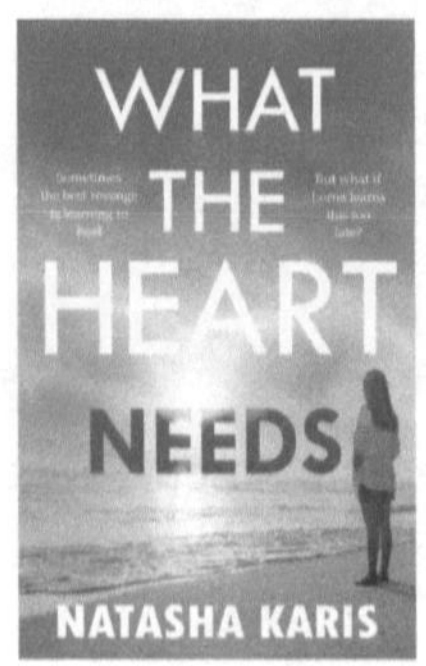

What The Heart Needs

Lorna Thomas has spent years trapped in the shadow of her daughter Sara's death. Grief has hardened into a relentless hunger for justice.

Tonight, she's finally ready to act.

But when she confronts the man she believes is responsible, a split-second revelation shatters everything she thought she knew. Instead of closure, Lorna finds herself pulled into the life of a haunted young man with secrets of his own.

As the truth unravels, Lorna is forced down an unexpected path paved not with revenge, but reckoning, forgiveness, and the raw ache of letting go.

***What the Heart Needs* is a gripping, emotional journey about the cost of love, the weight of guilt, and the strength it takes to choose healing over hurt.**

Check it out at: https://mybook.to/whattheheartneeds

The Sisters You Choose

It is near dark and pouring rain when Abbie Ellis visits her mother's grave for the first time.

Not to mourn or cry, for the last thing she wants is to forgive.

That night is the tenth anniversary of when her mother, the famous writer Gabrielle Ellis, took the lives of both Abbie's father and herself.

Finally ready to confront her past, Abbie hopes visiting the grave will unleash the anger she has held on to for too long.

But she is not alone.

A woman appears out of the shadows.

The stranger claims she knows Abbie and has a message from her mother.

Gabrielle wrote a secret book, only for her.

If she reads it, will Abbie get the answers she's hoped for all her life?

Will she finally learn what happened that fateful day?

A sweeping, emotional tale of wrong choices, of the power of friendship and enduring love that outlasts even death.

Check it out at: https://mybook.to/thesistersyouchoose

The Truth Between Us

Adaline and Andrew's marriage is all but over. They had thought their love would last a lifetime, yet they can't stand to stay in the same room for more than a minute.

Afraid to confront the truth, Adaline books a trip away alone to contemplate her next step, but Andrew surprises her with the suggestion he join her. Determined to break the stalemate and make a final decision either way, for the sake of their children, she agrees.

As they embark on a last chance holiday to Cyprus, Adaline reflects on her life, hoping to fix what went wrong. It's make or break time.

But the past contains much pain, and a secret threatens to ruin everything. Can they confront the truth that threatens to rip them apart and still salvage the relationship?

An emotional novel about love, loss and the redeeming power of hope.

Check it out: https://viewbook.at/thetruthbetweenus

The Breaking Of Dawn

Finding it impossible to express her opinion, Dawn Moloney spends her days doing what others tell her to. Taken for granted by her boss and friends, she can never find the right way to stand up to them. Nobody takes Dawn seriously, including herself.

Forced to move back to her childhood home after an attack leaves her bruised and broken, Dawn struggles to adjust.

When her mother suggests she try classes at a local centre for the unemployed, she reluctantly agrees. There, she meets Alayne Adams, who prefers to focus more on Dawn rather than what classes she is taking. Talking about herself is Dawn's worst nightmare, but if she wants to get better, she will have to learn.

Sometimes you have to step into the darkness to find your light, but can Dawn dive in and finally find the right words?

Check it out: https://viewbook.at/thebreakingofdawn

Stay (Previously published as The Initiates)

When the principal of Knockfarraig school suggests a series of detentions for some wayward sixth year students, teacher Alayne Adams volunteers. But the discovery of a note reveals one student intends to end their life.

Taking inspiration from a book based on ancient teachings, Alayne embarks on a series of life lessons that encourages each of them to discover ways to heal their pain.

Can she steer them onto a path that will change all their lives?

An emotional, heartfelt novel about the power of kindness and never giving up.

(Part of The Alayne Adams series)

The Initiation Of Alayne Adams

Torn between partying with her friends and doing the right thing, Alayne's life lacks any direction. Until an incident leaves her spiralling.

Left with nowhere to turn, Alayne struggles to find her way. But an encounter in a library opens up new possibilities and a chance to learn. Can Alayne change or will old habits prove too hard to resist?

A prequel novella to Stay (Part of The Alayne Adams Series)